LIVELY

by

La Juanda Huff Bishop

PublishAmerica

Baltimore

First printing

ISBN: 1-4137-1475-7
PUBLISHED BY PUBLISHAMERICA, LLLP
www.publishamerica.com
Baltimore

Printed in the United States of America

Dedications

This book is dedicated to my mother, Bernice Huff and my daughter, Anita who are now both deceased – the ones who continue to encourage me to follow my dreams and walk beside me whispering words of love and comfort to me as I face life's challenges and successes. I love and miss you both.

~ Your daughter and mother, La Juanda Bishop

Acknowledgements

First and foremost, I would like to thank God, whose love and mercy has brought me through many trials and tribulations and sustained me to accomplish my goals. To Debbie Clinton, friend and confidante, who continues to encourage me throughout our friendship. We shared tears of joy, sorrow and pain. You were happy for my accomplishments and sad for my defeats. My husband (Ted): we've gotten under each other's skin many times over the years, but our love prevailed and you will always be the love of my life for all time.

Penny, my computer whiz friend: without your friendship, I would probably be at square one. To Joe Ladensack, I will never forget your friendship and mentoring through many difficult times. Last but not least, Dorcas, who nurtured me as I grew into womanhood.

Other acknowledgements: Frances Smith, Bishop Paul and Carolyn Bynum, Kate Smith, Martha Jones, Debra Ingram, Mark Huff, Tracy Huff, Marcus McMillians, and Charles Brown (JR). Linda Grissom, Algia Huff (deceased), Marcus (JR), Justine, Joseph and Carolyn Tumpkin, Mildred Walton, Jeanette Grindle, my mother-in-law , Luevenia Brown, Frank Hazzard Holm, Andrea Little, Betty Harper, Ronald Hill, Don and Gwen Hotchkiss, Ms. Peggy Dean, Marilyn Anderson, Maurice Ingram, Nicole Clinton, Cora Stone, the entire staff at PublishAmerica for their personal and professional interest in this novel and all those who made an impact in my life…Thank You.

~ La Juanda (Huff) Bishop

LIVELY

The Secrets

La Juanda B.Bishop

Lively Jones, a sixteen-year-old girl living in the house with just her mother, and grandmother, two beautiful women who had hidden secrets from the past. What was their secret? What unspoken vow had they made to each other that did not allow them to mention their pasts? And the most puzzling secret of all. Who was her father?

On the night of the dance at the old mill by the Lake, she meets Randy Simmons, a popular boy from the exclusive part of town dubbed "High Town" by the less affluent citizens of the small suburban town. She falls quickly for the handsome captain of the football team.

When Lively tries to share some of her newfound emotions with Mama, she notices that it always seems to make her mother's thoughts drift away to some far-away place.

Her relationship has not only sparked an unexplainable sadness in Mama, but has also fueled the lust and rage of childhood friend Curtis Sampson. Even though he has only fabricated this relationship in his twisted mind, when Lively rebuffs his advances, he vows to make her pay.

A gripping tale of lust, love and secrets as the rich and powerful Franklin men get involved in clandestine relationships with Lively's mother and grandmother, and a happy ending as true love prevails.

CHAPTER ONE

Lively was fifteen years old. "Big for her age" Grandma said this every time she had sewn or bought her clothes. She had been saying this every year from the time that Lively was born. This is how she came by her strange name. Grandma loved to tell the story about how Lively came into the world not only squalling, but kicking and fighting. She had emerged screaming, fists flailing wildly and supposedly had given the attending doctor a hard right to his nose, causing him to exclaim "My goodness, Ella, you've got yourself a lively one here!" And so the name stuck.

Lively couldn't remember anything about her father. He was never mentioned and there were no pictures or evidence that he had ever existed. It had always been just herself, Mama, Grandma. That was the only world that she knew, except for occasional visits by the rats and roaches that showed their ugly selves every so often. She had long since ceased to be frightened by them, although as a little girl, she would cower in her bed under the covers as they skittered and slid across the torn linoleum in her little room. Once, a very bold rat had actually gotten under the covers as she slept and began nibbling on her big toe causing her to let out an ear-piercing scream, which jerked Mama and Grandma out of a deep sleep and from that night on, she slept in her sneakers and full dress battle armor to avoid being a full-course meal for them. And even when she avoided being eaten alive by them, there was the constant battle with bedbugs and mosquitoes.

Although the little house was in need of some very serious repair, the two older women kept it clean and orderly. There were always fresh flowers on the coffee table in the living room, which seemed to appear magically from somewhere, since there was no flower garden anywhere in the yard and the cracked linoleum throughout the house always glistened with the ever present can of Johnson Glo-Coat that grandma could just not live without.

Lively's mother and grandmother were beautiful and refined women. They walked with their heads held high, shoulders erect and were very soft-spoken and gentle. This was not a practiced behavior. You could tell that this aristocracy came from some long ago nobility. Lively remembered many occasions as they walked down the street to church or to the grocery store, she would see some of the women in the neighborhood stare at them with a mixture of envy and fascination. All the men in the neighborhood however would be staring at them in overt and covert admiration. Sometimes they were like little boys with their first crush on a girl and would act downright foolish in their attempts to be noticed by the two beautiful ladies. Mama and Grandma seemed to be oblivious to the stares and all they did was smile politely, nod their acknowledgments and continue on their way, dragging Lively with them.

When Lively was around nine or ten, she began to become aware of her surroundings. Mama would occasionally be given magazines from some of the "white folk" that she worked for. There would be *Good Housekeeping, House and Garden, McCall's and* a few fashion magazines. Lively would spend hours on end in her cubbyhole gazing at the pictures of the beautiful homes with their expensive furniture and draperies. The immaculate tiled kitchens with every appliance imaginable. The kitchens always had refrigerators with the doors opened, brimming with foods of which she had no idea what their names were. Then there would be the little girls' rooms, with their canopied beds, soft, floating curtains at the windows; beds piled high with fluffy stuffed animals and dolls. There was always a little blonde girl about her age poised on the bed with her starched ruffled dress on, hair shining with every strand in place, and eating a huge red delicious-looking apple.

Lively spent hour after hour gazing at these pictures. She would remove the little white girl from the pictures and in her mind; she would be sitting on the bed in the ruffled dress. She would then see herself going to the kitchen to the overloaded refrigerator and feasting on some imaginary morsel with an exotic name which only the rich and famous could pronounce and gorge herself on it and would feel full enough to not to have to lick her fingers afterwards.

Sometimes Lively would be so caught up in her dreams that she would not hear Mama or Grandma calling her until they stood in the doorway of her room and loudly called her back to the reality of her dreary little room, with its clean but tattered rug, frayed curtains and faded chenille bedspread. She would reluctantly put away the magazines and head to the kitchen for dinner, which mostly consisted of chicken, ground beef or liver. Nothing was as exotic or exciting as she had seen in the magazines. She realized even at that age that Mama worked hard to provide her with the meager comforts of their home and to try to insure that they had food on the table at every meal, but she still wished for a better life in a nice home, with a daddy going to and coming from work, while Mama stayed at home to take care of her home and family. This desire took root in her young mind and she vowed to find a way to have all the things that the little white girls in the magazines had.

CHAPTER TWO

These were the thoughts going through Lively's mind as she sat on the front steps that late autumn evening. The lone tree that stood in front of the house wore an array of bright fall colors. It swayed gently in the brisk autumn breeze and Lively hugged her arms about herself to keep the chill air from seeping through to her bones. All along the street, lights began to glow in houses that were a carbon copy of the one that she lived in. She saw smoke curling out of some of the chimneys and heard mothers calling their children in to wash up for dinner.

At the end of the block was old Mr. Pete's grocery store. He called it a grocery store, but he had almost every conceivable item you could think of. There was an array of odds and ends that always sat on their shelves from one year to the next. When a new shipment came in, they were moved to yet another shelf to make room for more worthless treasures. When old Mr. Pete ran out of space for the new shipment, he just concocted some sort of rickety shelf and transferred the old inventory to it.

Old Mr. Pete's store was also the meeting place for the unemployed men to gather. They would be sitting outside on the makeshift benches waiting for old Mr. Pete to open up his store to begin their day of discussions which ranged from who won the fight the night before to Felix Smith's new second-hand car to religion and politics. You could hear their loud voices and guffaws all the way down to the opposite end of the block.

Old Mr. Pete would be leaning in the doorway with his ever-present dingy apron on and a cigar that seemed to be the same length as the one that he had hanging from his lip the day before and the day before that. Every now and then someone would come to the store to buy something and old Mr. Pete would disappear inside the store and the loud talk would cease. When the transaction was done, he would reappear in the doorway and the conversation would pick up with the same loud intensity.

Lively looked toward the other end of the block and saw Curtis Sampson walking toward her house. She felt a frown of annoyance cross her face as she saw him looking hopefully at her. She wanted to jump up and run into the house, but Mama and Grandma had repeatedly told her to never treat company rudely, and even though she felt that Curtis Sampson was anything but company, she smiled graciously and prayed that he would not stay too long.

As he neared the step where she was sitting, his pimply face broke out in a smile, which revealed his uneven, yellowed teeth. He had an oversized plaid shirt on which had obviously been handed down from one of his many older brothers, who in turn probably got it from the Goodwill store. His faded jeans were about two sizes too small so they came to the tops of his run-over sneakers. Lively thought that she had never seen a more unattractive boy in her life. And the most sickening part of it was that Curtis had a huge crush on her and hung around like a bad cold.

"Hey there, L-L-Lively," he stuttered in high squeaky between-man-and-boy voice. "I thought that was you s-s-sitting there. Whatcha doing?"

She looked at him in disgust. What did it look like she was doing?

She had always hated answering questions that had only one obvious answer. But, she bit back the retort that was almost out of her mouth and answered as nicely as she could without letting on that she wished he would just head on back to where he had come from. "Nothing, Curtis, just sitting here minding my own business and *leaving everyone else's alone.* "

She didn't think that she had said anything funny, but suddenly Curtis flung his head back and let out a series of loud bellows like an elephant which she guessed to be laughter and snorted at the end of each bellow until she was sure that he would end up with snot bubbles blowing out of his nose. She shuddered repulsively at the thought. Her mind was whirling looking for an excuse to get rid of him, when he stopped laughing abruptly and gazed longingly at her for a few seconds. She could feel her irritation growing and asked him sharply, "What are you looking at me like that for, Curtis?"

He began shaking visibly and started clearing his throat and just about the time that she thought she might scream, he hesitatingly asked, "Didja hear about the dance they're having at the old mill by the lake on Sat'day night?" He stopped, looked at her some more before he continued. "I wuz jus' wondering if you wanna go wit' me?" Then he started shaking some more as he hung his head when he saw her quick look of revulsion.

She was just about to flatly refuse his offer, when she thought about Randy Simmons. Maybe Randy would be at the dance. Randy was one of the cutest boys in school. Randy also came from a very prominent family in town and she had a huge crush on him. But, although Randy had smiled at her many times and said hi to her as if they were equals, he had never shown any interest in her other than being polite. Randy was always dressed in expensive sweaters and pleated slacks that looked as if they cost more than her mother made in a month. He was also very popular with some of the prettiest and best-dressed girls in school, especially Terri Ann Morrison. Lively always felt dowdy in comparison to Randy and his crowd, although her clothes were always clean and pressed by Grandma. She knew that she was pretty. She had inherited Mama and Grandma's smooth taffy-colored complexions, up-tilted amber colored eyes and long, black naturally wavy hair. Her ancestors had been from Louisiana and had been Octoroon or something like that. Grandma had tried to explain it to her, but she hadn't paid much attention, but it accounted for her coloring and delicate features.

"H-h-m-m." She was yanked out of her reverie by Curtis clearing his throat again to get her attention and hopefully her acceptance of his offer of a date to the dance. She almost felt sorry for him, because he was so pitiful-looking, like an ugly puppy waiting for a pat on the head. She smiled sweetly and replied, "That's very nice of you, Curtis, to ask me to the dance, but I already have a date for that night, but if I see you there I'll save a dance for you."

She watched as Curtis' eyes glazed over with disappointment, then saw him quickly recover, square his shoulders with as much dignity as he could muster in his present state of dress, stutter "Thank You", and with the promise of seeing her on Saturday night, he turned and loped back in the direction that he had come from. She felt a moment of shame for the way she had refused him, but that was quickly replaced by the anticipation of hopefully seeing Randy Simmons at the dance.

The dance! How in the world was she going to convince Mama and especially Grandma to let her go to a dance? They had told her many times that she would not be allowed to go anywhere there was a mixed crowd until she was sixteen. Well, she would be sixteen in two months, so that had to count for something, didn't it? And she had always been a good girl, gotten good grades in school, didn't sass them, not only because she knew that Grandma would lecture her for the next five days on being a "disobedient child", but because she loved them dearly for the sacrifices that they made for her. She was given all the love that any child could want from a mother and father and they made sure she was clean and well fed and given lots of attention. Even though sometimes she wished for a father, it was not a driving force in her life, because Mama and Grandma made up for that.

She quickly got up from the steps and went into the house. She had heard the chicken as it had popped and sizzled as it hit the frying pan of hot grease and knew that supper would be ready soon. She also knew that Grandma liked for everyone to be at the table at the same time, so she could bless the food for all of them.

As she passed Grandma at the stove, she saw her look up and smile and say, "Hurry and wash your hands and come set the table. Your Mama should be home any minute now." Not wanting to displease Grandma in any way at this crucial moment in her life, Lively dashed to the tiny bathroom at the end of the hallway. Even though the bathroom smelled of Pine-sol and was clean and neat, with the plain white towels hanging on the silver towel bar and the little bathtub that was getting increasingly uncomfortable for Lively to lay back and relax in, she could still smell the faint odor of mildew and wrinkled her nose at the smell. She recalled how many times in the past when she had taken her "bubble bath" with the bubbles coming from a capful of dishwashing soap, she had fantasized about being a princess in her porcelain gold-footed tub, with ladies-in-waiting holding basins of warm fragrant water to pour over her as she lay surrounded by the fragrant bubbles.

She jerked herself out of her reverie when she heard a distinct bang of a pot on the stove, quickly washed her hands, dried them on the towel kept on the sink for that purpose, and hurried back to the kitchen.

She went to the counter where a stack of plates in assorted colors and patterns were arranged neatly. These were Mama's "everyday dishes". She had a beautiful set of china and silverware that she had in a locked cabinet for holidays and company. As she began setting out three of the most closely matched plates and completely mismatched silverware, the back door opened and Mama walked in.

Lively looked at her mother and as usual was awestruck by her beauty. The brisk wind had caused her skin to glow, making her look much younger than her thirty-five years. Her slim nose was slightly tilted on the end and her light amber-colored eyes sparkled and crinkled shut when she smiled. She had very high cheekbones, which came from somebody somewhere being "part Cherokee" according to another attempt by Grandma to teach her about her heritage. She had her hair pulled back in a ponytail making her eyes take on a feline appearance. When she smiled, she showed the most intriguing dimples in her cheeks. Her smile was very engaging and it was usually visible. Lively could not understand how any man could have resisted her mother's beauty and why she had been alone all of these years. She remembered as a small child she would ask Mama and Grandma about her father and they both would give her the same answer, "When you're old enough, we'll tell you." Eventually, she just stopped asking and accepted that it was just Grandma, Mama and herself.

Mama had a large grocery bag in her arms and she handed it to Lively."This is for you, Hunny." Mama's pet name for her had always been "Hunny" because of the color of her skin and she said that Lively was as sweet as honey.

Lively assumed that the bag was filled with the customary magazines, which made her all too aware of her surroundings. She took it to her room and put it in the corner of her closet for later perusal.

Lively went back to the kitchen, where Mama and Grandma were already sitting at the table waiting for her to join them. Grandma already had her hands folded ready to pray over the meal and as Lively sat down, she began the ritual, which usually lasted about ten minutes. The food was usually lukewarm by the time they began eating it. Normally, Lively couldn't wait for Grandma to finish so she could tear into her food, but tonight she was glad for the extra time as she pondered on how to approach her mother and grandmother with the subject of the dance.

CHAPTER THREE

After supper, while Mama and Grandma sat in the living room watching a favorite television program and discussing its characters and events, Lively did the dishes. This was about the only chore that was given to her. The dishes and keeping her room cleaned. Mama and Grandma were more concerned with her homework and school projects. They said that through her good grades, she would be able to go to college and get an education, so that she would not have to work in people's homes or have to wait to be age sixty-five to get her Social Security check like Grandma. They wanted her to have a career first, husband and child later.

When Lively finished the dishes, she went into the living room with one of her schoolbooks to join Mama and Grandma. She pretended to be reading, while listening to them talk and waiting for the right moment to broach the subject of the dance.

Finally, they both stopped talking and began to watch the show and Lively's heart began to pound as she pondered how to begin. As she opened her mouth to speak, one of the characters on the screen, a teenaged girl, began telling her parents that she was pregnant. She was only about fourteen years old. Mama and Grandma were gazing intently at the screen, Grandma with a frown of disapproval on her face and Mama with another look on hers. Lively could not decipher the look, but it appeared to be a look of melancholy and a kind of sadness. Lively had seen this look on Mama's face many times over the years and although she did not know why, she felt sad for her mother at these moments. It was if she would not be aware of where she was and lost in time somewhere in the past. Lively knew tonight was not a good night to bring up the subject of the dance.

The next morning though, Lively sprang out of bed as soon as she heard the shrill call of the alarm clock announcing that it was six o'clock and time to get up for school. She hurried down the short expanse of the hallway to the tiny bathroom, and after a quick sponge bath, dressed and galloped to the kitchen for breakfast. Mama was in the kitchen at the stove, stirring a pot of oatmeal. She and Grandma had agreed that since Grandma cooked the evening meals and took care of the household chores, Mama would prepare breakfast while Grandma 'slept in'.

"Good morning, Hunny," Mama said as she peeked into the oven at the homemade biscuits that were almost golden brown. "How's my big girl this morning?" Lively loved her mother, but she wished sometimes that she would not talk to her the same way that she had when she was little. Goodness! Couldn't she see the breasts that had sprung up on her chest and the curves that she was developing? But, she only answered, "Fine, Mama", and sat at the table.

Lively watched her mother as she moved around the tiny kitchen. She moved with such elegance, and even at this early hour, with her hair mussed and in her old pink bathrobe, she was beautiful. Lively once again began thinking about her mother. She was too beautiful to be alone. What was the mystery surrounding her past that was never talked about? One day she would tell her mother that she was "old enough" to know, but for right now she had bigger fish to fry.

Her mother spooned the hot, bubbling oatmeal into two bowls, split two of the huge biscuits down the middle and slathered the pieces with margarine and put them on a separate plate and placed everything on the table. Then she sat down across from Lively and began to pray. Fortunately Mama's prayers didn't go on and on like Grandma's did, so the food was still nice and warm as they began to eat.

"Mama?" Lively began. Her mother looked at her expectantly. Lively cleared her throat and decided that the best thing to do was get this over with as quickly and painlessly as possible. At least, there was only Mama sitting there looking at her. If she could convince Mama about the dance, then it would be up to Mama to win Grandma over. "Mama", she continued. "There's a dance at the old mill by the lake this weekend and some of my friends from school are going to it and wanted to know if I could go to it". She looked at her mother and thought she saw a flicker of sadness cross her delicate features. Her mother had a far-away look in her eyes and seemed to not be in their little kitchen, but in some secret place.

"Mama, what's wrong?" Lively queried. Her mother slowly brought her gaze back to her daughter's face and seemed to be trying to focus on her and what she was saying. "Mama, did you hear me?"

"Yes, Hunny, I heard you. I was just thinking of the conversation that we had about what age we would allow you to go to mixed parties."

"But Mama, there will be chaperones from school there and of course some parents will be there. Mama, you and Grandma could even come and volunteer as chaperones," she offered, even though she really didn't want either one of them there.

Mama looked at her speculatively for a few seconds that seemed like hours before saying doubtfully, "I don't know dear. I really don't think that a girl of fifteen should go to parties with boys that I don't know."

"But, Mama, you know Curtis Sampson. He even asked me to go with him," she countered.

Her mother nodded, thinking of the homely boy who sometimes came around to talk to her daughter. She had noticed how Curtis looked longingly at her daughter as if she were a priceless gem. She also remembered how Mother and she had discussed how they hoped that no romance developed between her daughter and Curtis. This was not the future son-in-law that she wanted for her daughter. She wanted Lively to have a much better life than she had. She knew of the Sampson family. Mr. Sampson was a man known for his voracious appetite of drink and womanizing. He was also known for his abusiveness to his wife and children. Not that she blamed Curtis for the sins of his father. Lord knew the child had enough to live through without more criticism coming from her. She just wanted more for her only child. So, she asked, "Did you promise to be his date for the dance?"

Lively gave her mother a wide-eyed look of horror, as she exclaimed, "No way, Mama! I told him that I was too young to be going on dates. But truthfully, Mama even if I were old enough to date, it sure wouldn't be with Curtis Sampson. Have you seen how he dresses, Mama? And his teeth are so crooked and yellow. He looks like a Jack-o- lantern."

Her mother suppressed a laugh, as she gently chided her daughter for talking about poor Curtis. "Hunny, that boy has had a hard life. I know you've heard about Mr. Sampson's treatment of his family. But, you've said yourself that Curtis is smart and gets good grades and is planning to go to college, somehow. So, even though he is unattractive to you, he is still a human being and should be treated with respect." Mama ended her speech with an intent look at her daughter as if she was saying one thing about Curtis, but was thinking of someone else

Lively felt chastened and apologized to her mother. "I'm sorry, Mama, I know Curtis has a pitiful life. And he is smart, but I'm not thinking about boys right now," she lied. *Only one*, she said to herself as she thought of the well-dressed, popular boy with the curly hair and dimples in his cheeks.

She watched as her mother hungrily attacked the oatmeal, dipping the biscuit into it and savoring the sweet, buttery flavor. She seemed to have forgotten the conversation that they were having, so Lively hurriedly asked again, "Mama, what about the dance?"

Her mother finished chewing the bite of bread, swallowed and answered slowly, "We'll see. Let me think about it. I'll let you know tonight."

Lively knew this meant that Mama was going to consult Grandma on the subject, first. It seemed that Mama was always consulting Grandma on any decision. Lively couldn't understand why a thirty-five year old woman could not make a decision without her mother's approval, but this is how it had always been with Mama and Grandma.

CHAPTER FOUR

By the next morning when Mama still hadn't given her an answer about the party, Lively began to feel a sense of desperation. She hurried through her morning bath, brushed he teeth, dressed in her best blue dress and black flat shoes and went to the kitchen at breakneck speed. She just had to get an answer from Mama this morning. Yesterday morning as she had been walking to her locker, Randy Simmons had smiled at her and asked her how she was doing. He had never done that before and she spent the whole day elated by the possibility that he might actually be noticing her.

Mama was at the stove again and gave her the customary smile and greeting as she pulled the crisp bacon dripping with grease from the skillet and laid it in a row on a paper towel to drain. Lively gave her a kiss on the cheek and asked if there was anything she could do to help.

Mama looked at her in surprise, but shook her head in refusal. She said that everything was done and ready to be served. She brought the plates of bacon, eggs and pancakes over to the table. She returned to the counter to get the two glasses of milk she had poured for them and handed Lively's to her. She sat down across from her, murmured the now familiar prayer for the "food they were about to receive" and began to eat. Lively waited to see if she was going to say something to her about the dance and when she didn't, she began to slowly eat her own breakfast.

Mama began talking about her day's events and the extra work she was going to do because the Franklins' son was coming home for a visit with his wife and two children, so Mama would have to work later that night making sure that everything would be ready for their arrival.

Lively listened absently as Mama rambled on about the Franklins for awhile, then when she heard Mama's voice trail off in mid-sentence, she listened closely to hear her words because Mama's voice sounded suddenly sad. "…And Greg Jr.'s other children should be about thirteen and ten now." Who was Greg Jr.? And why should Mama care how old his children were? Why should she sound so sad and lost talking about these white people that she worked for? Other children? What did that mean? She was just about to ask, when suddenly Mama brightened, remembered her daughter sitting across from her and asked her what she would be doing in school that day.

Good. This was the opening that Lively had been waiting for. "Well, Mama, as a matter of fact, Janelle and I were going to get together this afternoon after school and choose what we're wearing to the dance." Janelle Truesdell had been her best friend since kindergarten. Although her family had more money than Lively's and Janelle lived in an upper class neighborhood, she had always treated Lively as her equal and never showed anything but love and friendship to her over the years. "That is if you say I can go, Mama," she added.

Ella looked at her daughter's expectant face, filled with anticipation, so like her father's and her heart melted. *I guess I can give in to her this time,* she thought. *After all, you're only young once and I don't want her to lose out on her youth and fun the way that I did.* She had always secretly resented how strict her own mother and father had been. Maybe if they hadn't been so strict and had helped her learn about life by allowing her the freedom of having friends and boyfriends, things wouldn't have happened the way that they did. *I mustn't think about what if...I must think of the present,* she scolded herself silently.

So, she smiled indulgently at her daughter and said, "Okay, I'm going to trust you to go to the party and come home at ten o'clock. You must promise to be careful and be home by ten, okay?"

Lively's face broke out in a wide smile, as she jumped up and ran to the other side of the table grabbed Mama and hugged her tightly, laughing excitedly as she exclaimed, "Oh, thank you, thank you Mama! I promise to be home at ten and yes, I will be careful. I can't wait to get to school and tell Janelle the good news!"

With that flung over her shoulder she dashed out of the door. Mama sat at the table with a worried expression on her face. *Now, I've got to tell Mama my decision. I know that she will not be happy, but I made a choice for my daughter's happiness, for once. Like she should have done years ago,* she thought bitterly. With that thought in mind, she stood up, squared her shoulders and left the kitchen ready to do battle with her mother.

CHAPTER FIVE

The weather on the night of the dance was unseasonably warm. A gentle breeze was blowing through the leaves on the sycamore trees and the full moon overhead was as shiny as a new silver dollar. Wispy clouds floated by the moon slowly and the bullfrogs down by the lake croaked in tune with the music coming from inside the old mill. Tinkling laughter and deep bellows could be heard coming from the porch outside the mill as Lively and Janelle hurried toward the gaiety.

The two girls were walking arm in arm, their faces alight with the anticipation of fun and the possibility of a romantic encounter. Lively was the taller of the two girls. Janelle was petite and feminine, while Lively was taller and large-boned. This was not a negative thing as she was very well proportioned with long shapely legs, a small waist and well-rounded hips. Her breasts were ample and even at this age, her figure promised to be perfect. Tonight she was dressed in a cream-colored satin slip-dress that reached to her ankles. Her soft, black hair was curled and piled high at the crown of her head and held in place by a rhinestone clip that her mother had let her wear. She had pleaded with Grandma for her pearl necklace and tiny pearl earrings. Grandma grudgingly gave them to her, but did not voice her disapproval and Lively wondered what her mother had said to Grandma to keep her silent, because Grandma was always outspoken. She had on a pair of low-heeled sandals on her bare feet that she had spent about two hours on filing the nails to perfection and then polishing them with a mauve-colored nail enamel. She had put on some lipstick and mascara, after leaving the house. She knew that Grandma would draw the line there and she didn't want to do anything to impede her going to the dance. She felt pretty and glanced affectionately at her friend who had spared nothing in her closet, so that she could look good for the dance.

As they neared the entrance to the dance, a shadowy figure came from the side of the mill. At first they were frightened, but it didn't take long for Lively to recognize the familiar lope of Curtis Sampson.

"Hey, Curtis," she said, and thought, *I hope he isn't planning on hanging around me all night. That's all I need!* She took in his appearance noticing his pitiful attempt at dressing for the dance. He had on an oversized three-piece suit that had most likely belonged to an older brother. It had a dark blue coat with gray wrinkled slacks and a vest that had matched them at one time, but now was slightly discolored. His white shirt and blue polka dot tie gave him a clownish appearance. His slicked down hair had a large side part in it and the grease was so thick on it that it could be seen even in the shadows. His face brightened at the sight of her and she was rewarded with his yellowed grin.

"Evenin' Lively. Glad to see you could make it to the dance." He did not even acknowledge Janelle's presence; he just kept staring at Lively and said, "You sure lookin' pretty tonight. Are you still gonna dance wit' me like you promised?"

Lively could barely suppress the uncontrollable shudder that went through her as she replied, "Sure, Curtis, but first Janelle and I need to get inside to our dates."

Curtis' head snapped toward Janelle as if seeing her for the first time. "Oh, hel-l-o Janelle," he stuttered." Okay, I'll see you later, Lively. By the way, who's your date for tonight?'

Lively hesitated briefly while her mind scrambled to think of someone, and then she recovered quickly, "He's someone from out of town, a friend of Janelle's date. You wouldn't know him," she said as she nudged Janelle in the side slightly as she spoke.

"Okay, I'll be back for my dance," he said as he sauntered off toward the open door of the mill.

"What was that all about?" Janelle asked as she looked curiously at Curtis' retreating figure.

"Oh, nothing, I saw him the other day and he told me about the dance and asked me if I would save him a dance." Lively wasn't about to tell her friend, even if they were best friends that the only boy who had asked her to the dance was Curtis Sampson. So, she smiled brightly and pulled her friend quickly toward the dance. "Come on, there's a party going on!" They laughed and hurried into the mill.

Once a long time ago the mill had been a thriving paper mill. It was bought at the turn of the century by a man name Eustis Franklin, who had come from Europe. His family had been some sort of Royalty and due to a scandal of some sort, Eustis had been granted his inheritance and exiled to America.

Eustis had scouted different locations before settling here and after many meetings with other affluent citizens of that era, bought the paper mill and through his knowledge of business and his monetary assets, he turned the mill into one of the most profitable businesses in the region. The mill remained a flourishing business for several decades, before finally closing and sitting dormant until Greg Franklin, Sr. decided to donate it to the town to use as a banquet hall.

Tonight, it was decorated in gold and white. The long tables on one side of the room were adorned in white heavily starched tablecloths, gold platters and bowls loaded with barbecued chicken, potato salad, macaroni salad, finger sandwiches, baked beans and an array of pastries and cakes. Another table at the end of the room was filled with plates, bowls, silverware, drinking glasses and napkins. In the center of yet another table were several punch bowls filled with assorted flavors and colors of chilled sparkling punch. Lively saw several students that she knew from school standing there with glasses in their hands, talking, laughing or just watching everyone as they passed by.

The dance floor gleamed from the polishing that it had received earlier that day and there was a sprinkling of dancers on the floor gyrating to the beat of a fast-paced song played by the five-member band that Lively recognized as some of the members from the school band. She stood by the doorway with her friend Janelle with excited eyes as she watched all the fun and excitement swirl around her. She had never seen so many people outside of church and certainly not in such a festive mood. She felt her own pulse begin to race as she began to get caught up in the excitement.

Janelle grabbed her hand and pulled her toward the table for a drink. "Come on, let's go mingle with the crowd," she said excitedly. Lively let herself be guided to the table, feeling an overwhelming shyness come over her at being among so many people, especially boys. When they reached the table, she picked up a glass and filled it with a burgundy colored drink from one of the punch bowls, being careful not to spill it on herself. She turned to watch the people on the dance floor. She noticed that Janelle was talking to a boy that she recognized from school, then turn to her to say that she was going to dance with him. Lively gave a small smile and watched as her friend sailed out to the floor with the boy, laughing and saucily tossing her head as she smiled and flirted with the boy. Lively wished that she had learned to talk and flirt with boys, but Mama and Grandma had never allowed her to be around them enough to learn that skill. She momentarily envied her friend, but quickly shook away that feeling, ashamed of herself. Janelle was her friend, for heaven's sake! She pasted a smile on her face and pretended to be absorbed with watching the dancers.

"Well, hello, lovely lady," a voice whispered to her over her shoulder. She spun around, splashing some of the ruby-colored liquid onto the floor as she did. Fortunately, none of it spilled onto her dress. Her wide eyes were focused on the face that belonged to the voice. Randy Simmons was standing there smiling at her! He looked so handsome in a blue pinstriped double-breasted suit. He had on a red Arrow shirt and red silk tie. He looked as if he had stepped straight from a fashion magazine. His curly hair hung to his shoulders in rich waves, and his smile was gorgeous with the whitest, most even teeth she had ever seen. She couldn't believe he was actually standing in front of her.

She wasn't aware that she had been openly staring at him until he asked, "What's the matter, did I suddenly grow horns?" He gently laughed at her confusion.

She knew he was awaiting her response and her mouth opened and closed several times before she breathlessly answered, "H-h-hi, Randy." She was ashamed of the way she stuttered over her greeting and fought to compose herself before speaking again. "I didn't see you come in."

"I was already here. I was just in the back room making sure that everything was going as planned," he explained.

She knew that Randy was the president of the student body and on so many committees at school that it was natural for him to be in charge of tonight's events.

"I saw you standing over here all alone and as chairperson of this event, it is my duty to insure that everyone enjoys themselves and not stand around looking lost and not having the time of their life." He looked at her as if measuring her to see if she were having a good time.

She felt a wave of disappointment course through her. He was only here talking to her because it was his duty! Apparently her face must have reflected her disappointment, because he hastily continued. "Of course, when there is such a beautiful damsel such as yourself in distress, it's more of a pleasure than a responsibility."

She gave him a bright smile displaying the deep dimples in

her cheeks. He saw them and commented, "And since I don't know your name, I christen thee, Lady Dimples.

Lively could not control herself and burst into laughter at his nickname for her. Then she sobered as she saw him looking at her intently again. "May I have this dance, Madam," he asked.

For a moment, she felt panic. She did not know how to dance, except for the few times that she and Janelle had pretended to be dancing with boys in her room. But, she let him lead her to the dance floor, any way. She was glad for the crowd of people who surged to the floor and was even gladder that it was a slow tune, so she could lean into Randy in case she stumbled. She looked up at him as he softly began to sing the words of the song that was playing in her ear. He smiled down at her and held her closer to him as they continued dancing, their bodies a perfect fit it was if they had always danced together. Out of the corner of her eye, she saw Curtis Sampson leering at them contemptuously. On the other side of the room, she spotted Terri Ann Morrison staring open-mouthed at them as she leaned over and whispered to her friends. But, she was too caught up in the magic of the moment to care.

Just then, she felt a hard tap on her shoulder. It was Curtis Sampson.

He made an effort to appear like some romantic figure from a novel as he bowed low and asked if he could cut in. She was about to flatly refuse, when Randy smiled politely and said, "Of course, Curtis. If the lady wishes to dance with you", he added.

Lively could not think of a viable excuse to give to Curtis, so she just smiled indulgently and switched partners. As Randy walked away, he said over his shoulder, "Treat the lady kindly, my man. I wouldn't want anything to happen to her." Lively watched his retreating back for a few seconds, before she was roughly grabbed around the waist by Curtis and dragged to the middle of the floor. She looked into his face at the glittering eyes that seemed to try to devour her. He wore a lascivious grin on his face and she turned her face away from the putrid breath coming from his mouth. She thought she detected the slight smell of alcohol on him, but wasn't sure. He started dancing clumsily with her, dipping and bowing her in a pitiful attempt to look like an experienced dancer. More than once, she had to hold on tightly to him to keep from tumbling in an ungraceful heap on the floor. She saw other couples on the dance floor staring and snickering at them as he propelled her all around the floor, occasionally bumping into the other dancers. She had never been so embarrassed in her life. Terri Ann Morrison and her friends were laughing loudly and pointing at them.

Finally, the song ended, but Curtis would not release his hold on her. She began squirming trying to get out of his grasp. She began to feel a sense of panic as he tightened his grip. "Let me go, Curtis!" she demanded.

He held her in his death-grip and his foul-smelling breath came at her in waves as he leaned his face toward her. Oh, No! He surely wasn't going to kiss her!! He was so repulsive and the thought of his wet, stinking mouth was too much for her. She began struggling wildly in his grasp.

"I think the lady is finished dancing for now, don't you, Curtis?"

Randy was there at her side. His voice was low, but you could hear the venom dripping from it. He firmly extricated Curtis' arms from around her and after the two men stared at each other with the promise of vindication in both of their looks, Randy escorted her to the refreshment table. Just then, Janelle came hurrying over to the table. She looked at her friend's flushed face.

"Are you okay?" she asked. "It looked as though Curtis was giving you a hard time." Lively nodded to her that she was okay. Janelle looked from her to Randy and a smile spread across her face. "I guess you are," she said with a wink and skittered back across the floor to the young man that had held her attention since the beginning of the evening.

She looked up at Randy and said, "Thank you for rescuing me from Curtis. I have known him all of my life, but tonight, there was something different in his attitude. I was seriously afraid for a few seconds."

"No problem," he smiled down at her. "I love rescuing beautiful ladies in distress from fiery dragons. It adds some spice to a gentleman's life."

Then he asked her if she would like to go get a plate of food with him and she found herself being led by the arm. She couldn't believe it. Here she was with the most handsome guy at the dance and he seemed to be totally enraptured by her. Tomorrow this would seem like a dream, but tonight it was very real and she was speechless. After heaping their plates, they found a quiet corner to sit and eat.

After eating quietly for a while, Randy began asking her about her life. She felt so comfortable around him that she began to talk animatedly about her mother and grandmother, her dreams of college and a better life for her family. She had wanted to become a doctor or lawyer, but hers was a more creative nature and she had become avidly interested in designing. She wanted to get as far away from her drab neighborhood as possible. Her mother would never have to clean houses for people again and Grandma could go on a cruise with some of her elderly friends. As she talked, she could actually feel herself in this capacity and Randy did not miss the gleam of determination in her eyes. He felt that he had never seen any woman as beautiful and exciting as this one. He felt a strange longing surge through him as he took in her beautiful light amber eyes, the two dimples that appeared in her cheeks when she talked or smiled. He was so mesmerized by her, and he did not know why. His life was so different from hers. He was not born with a silver spoon in his mouth, but he was from a very affluent family in the community. His father was the superintendent of all the schools in the district and his mother was dean of the local city college. He felt an overwhelming feeling of protectiveness toward her that he could not explain.

The band started playing another slow song and Randy was about to ask Lively if she like to dance, when Terri Ann Morrison sashayed up to him. "I've been looking for you," she pouted prettily. "You haven't asked me to dance yet tonight." She looked accusingly at Lively before turning back to Randy with a petulant smile. "Come on," she said grabbing his hand and pulling him up before he had a chance to answer. He threw an apologetic glance at Lively and trotted off behind Terri Ann to the dance floor.

Lively sat watching the pair on the floor, noticing the way Terri Ann moved against Randy provocatively, smiling up at him and casting a smug look in Lively's direction.

When Lively could no longer stand to witness her antics, she turned her attention toward the open doorway. She saw Curtis Sampson slouching there watching her with an angry expression on his face. When he started toward where she sat, she jumped up and escaped to the bathroom. She stood in front of the mirror, straightening her dress and freshening her makeup. The door opened and Janelle entered.

"Whew!" her friend exclaimed. "I haven't had a moment to catch my breath since we got here."

"I know," said Lively. "You've been on the dance floor through at least ten songs. You must be dying of thirst after all that dancing."

"Dying of thirst and starving," Janelle replied. "But, what about you and Mr. Handsome? Every time I do look your way, he seems to be with you. And when he isn't with you, he's standing somewhere nearby watching you."

Lively felt a flush creep across her face. "Oh, you're just exaggerating. You know how you're famous for your vivid imagination."

"I am not exaggerating! He is definitely interested in you, girl. And if I were in your shoes, I'd be out there right now trying to keep Miss Hot Pants from getting him in her clutches!"

she said, facing Lively with her legs spread-eagled and her hands on her hips.

Lively smiled patiently at her friend as she continued applying lipstick to her mouth. She had gotten used to her friend's dramatics over the years. She picked up her purse and followed Janelle out of the bathroom. When she returned to her still empty seat, Curtis Sampson was nowhere in sight.

CHAPTER SIX

Lively looked at her wristwatch. Nine-thirty! Where had the evening gone? She looked around for her friend. She saw her on the dance floor, slow-dragging with the same boy she had been dancing with all evening. She had her eyes closed and her head was resting on his shoulder. Lively hated to disturb her, but she knew that she had to be home by ten or Mama would never trust her again.

She walked over to the spot where Janelle was dancing and tapped her lightly on the shoulder. Janelle looked at her for a second as if she didn't recognize her, then she smiled at her.

"Janelle, it's nine-thirty! We've got to be getting home!' Lively said frantically.

Her friend looked at her as if she had lost her mind. "Are you kidding, the party is just getting started!'

"But, I promised Mama that I'd be home at ten," Lively protested. She was getting annoyed at her friend's lack of concern. She had already told her earlier that she could not stay out past ten o'clock.

"I'm sure that your mother and grandmother are in bed fast asleep by now. They probably won't even know that you're not home," said Janelle, trying to change her mind.

Just as Lively was about to answer, Randy Simmons walked up to them. "Hey, I couldn't help overhearing your conversation, and I have a solution for both of you. He looked hopefully at Lively as he continued. "How about I escort Lively home and Janelle can stay here until she's ready to leave?"

Janelle answered quickly, "Yeah, that's a great idea! How about it, Lively?" she asked, trying not to look too hopeful.

Lively gave her friend a not too pleased look, making a mental note to let her know tomorrow how she felt about this breach of promise, and politely accepted Randy's offer. He told her that he needed to let the committee chairman know that he would be gone for a while and then he came back and offered Lively his arm. As they walked to the door, she saw Terri Ann staring at them with hateful eyes, and she returned the look with a smug smile and purposefully smiled up at Randy, dimpling as she did so.

When they stepped outside, the night air had a slight chill to it. She shivered involuntarily and Randy saw it. He unbuttoned his blazer and gently placed it around her shoulders. "Is that better?" he asked. She nodded "yes" and they began to walk toward her neighborhood. They were both silent for a while, enjoying the moonlit night, listening to the bullfrogs and the occasional barking of a distant dog.

He reached for her hand and smiled down at her upturned face. All too soon, they reached her house. He looked at her and although she couldn't see his face in the shadows, she felt the tender look that he gave her.

"I want you to know that I really enjoyed spending time with you, tonight. I felt as if I'd known you all of my life. Do you think we can see each other again?" he asked.

She was glad that he couldn't see her face in the dark as it was burning with embarrassment. "I   I don't think so. My mother won't allow me to date until I'm sixteen and that won't be until two months from now," she explained in a small voice.

She felt his fingers under her chin as he lifted her face up to his. He smiled and said, "Well, that's not that far away from now. But, I think we can find a way to see each other off and on until then, don't you?"

Her heart started to pound as he leaned down toward her. She held her breath. He was going to kiss her! When his lips touched hers, they were soft and his breath was warm and sweet. He tasted like peppermint. He wore a cologne that was heady in its fragrance and she was mesmerized by it. Although she had never been kissed by any boy except a distant cousin and certainly not this kind of kiss, she knew that she would never want to be kissed by anyone else.

Then Randy released her and smiled at her again. "Goodnight, Lady Dimples," he said and turned and walked back toward the old mill. She watched him disappear into the darkness and turned slowly and went into the house.

As the front door closed behind her, she did not hear the rustling in the tall Johnson grass in the field beside her house. A dark figure was lurking there watching as she kissed Randy Simmons. It was Curtis Sampson. As he turned to leave, he muttered one word. "Bitch!"

CHAPTER SEVEN

Mama sat down across the table from Lively the next morning at breakfast. She spooned the still steaming scrambled eggs onto her plate. She sprinkled salt and pepper on them and tasted them. She took a sip of coffee from her favorite cup, as she looked at Lively. "Did you have a nice time at the dance last night?" she asked, putting the cup down.

Lively looked up from her plate of food and smiled at Mama. "Oh, yes, it was great," she answered, trying to not sound too excited. Mama's keen mind had always been able to look straight into her soul, it seemed, since she was a small child.

"Well, are you going to tell me about it?" Mama asked her. Lively knew she would have to tell Mama about the dance. She had not stopped to talk much to her and Grandma when she arrived home last night. They had looked up expectantly when she entered the living room to tell them that she was home, but Lively's mind was still whirling from the emotions evoked by her first kiss. She wanted to go straight to her room and lie in bed and relive the night's events while they were still fresh in her mind. Her lips were still tingling from the pressure of Randy's mouth and she felt all warm and soft inside. She just didn't want to share the aftermath of these feelings with anyone right then.

"Well, there really isn't that much to tell". She hesitated and continued. "There were a lot of people there. Janelle spent the whole evening dancing with a boy named Thomas. They had a five-piece band from school and the food was good."

Mama looked at her keenly, then queried, "What about you? Did you dance with anyone?"

Lively knew that Mama was not going to let up on the questioning without getting some answers from her, so she said, "Yes, I did dance with that awful Curtis Sampson. He acted horribly, Mama. He wouldn't let me go when the song ended and I had to try to push him away. And he tried to kiss me! Can you believe that? It would have been worse than kissing a slimy frog! If Randy Simmons hadn't come to my rescue, I don't know what would have happened."

Her mother looked up suddenly when she heard Randy Simmons' name, not because Lively said it, but because of the way her daughter's voice softened when she said it, almost like a purr.

"Who is Randy Simmons?" she wanted to know. She remembered hearing the name Simmons before. Some affluent people who lived on the other side of town. She didn't think that Lively was talking about the same people.

"You remember him Mama. We talked about him yesterday, remember? "He's this really cute boy that goes to my school. His father is the superintendent of schools and his mother is the dean at City College. He's the President of the senior class and very popular!" she said, excitedly. Mama seemed to be somewhere else a lot these days. Lively began to worry about her short attention span. Was Mama getting senile so young?

Mama saw her daughter's worried glance and smiled at her. Lively looked so much like her father. Oh, how she had loved him with the same innocence. She knew that by looking at Lively's animated face that this was more than just a passing fancy for this Randy Simmons. "Did he dance with you last night, too?" she wanted to know.

"Yes. Two times, Mama, then when I was ready to come home and Janelle wasn't, he walked me home!" Lively was so absorbed in her own happiness that she did not see the frown that crossed over Mama's face. But, seeing her daughter so happy, Mama found it hard to scold her. After all, it all sounded so innocent, but she reminded herself to talk to her daughter later about strange boys walking her home at night

Lively quickly finished her breakfast and bolted toward her room. She wanted to finish her weekly cleaning and do her homework so that she could call Janelle to gossip about the dance last night.

Mama sat at the table after Lively had left the room looking at the wall. She was remembering a time too, when she was young. It was a time of innocence and love. Her thoughts revisited a place and time eighteen years ago.

Ella Jones stood at the white double doors of the massive house. She looked at the address on the piece of paper that Mother had given her to make sure she was at the right address. Her hand shook slightly as she lifted the heavy brass knocker and tapped it lightly three times. After what seemed an interminable wait, the door opened and a tall, blonde boy about her age looked warily at her. "Yes, may I help you?" he asked squinting down at her with the grayest eyes she had ever seen.

She found her voice and answered, "My name is Ella. I'm the new housekeeper. I hope this is the right address"

The tall boy smiled at her and asked her to come in. "Right this way. Mom is in the study having tea and I think she's expecting you." He stopped in front of a closed door and tapped lightly. A haughty voice on the other side of the door invited him to enter and Ella followed closely behind him, her heart in her throat.

The voice demanded, "Come over here so I can see you. Why are you hiding behind Gregory like that?"

Ella stepped timidly from behind the tall boy named Gregory to face her new employer. She looked at the silver-haired lady sitting in a Queen Ann chair, holding a flowered teacup in her hand and looking over her jeweled framed glasses at her.

The lady looked her up and down, then stated flatly, "I was expecting someone a little older. What's your name, child and how old are you?"

Ella felt as if she would faint, she was shaking so hard. "M-m-y name is Ella, M'aam and I'm seventeen, going on eighteen." The lady was staring at her so sternly that Ella found herself involuntarily retreating toward the door. She could see the tall boy looking at her with a teasing gleam in his eye and she felt herself relaxing a bit. His look told her that his mother's bark was worse than her bite.

The lady looked at her for several seconds, as she continued sipping her tea, then asked brusquely, "Can you follow orders? What about cooking? Your mother tells me that you are a good housekeeper and learn quickly. I hope so, because I will only accept the best. Gregory." Her voice softened as she called to her son. "Take her into the kitchen and introduce her to Miriam. Tell her that this is the new housekeeper and she is to train her right!" With a fling of her jeweled hands in the direction of the door, Ella was hired and dismissed to her duties all at once.

She followed the boy named Gregory out into the hallway and he turned and smiled at her. He was quite a handsome boy, with white even teeth, a wide, friendly, smile, devilish gray eyes and a well-formed body. She could tell that he was very athletic. "Don't be frightened of Mom," he said to her. "Once you get used to her and she gets used to you, you will find that she has a soft heart that she doesn't want anyone to know about. I'm not saying that she will not yell and scare the bejesus out of you, but she is reasonable and fair. Except when it comes to me. Then she becomes as protective as a mother bear," he ended with a laugh.

Ella made no comment as the woman's attitude and blunt manner of speaking spoke of anything but kindness. Still, Ella found herself smiling at the young man. She liked him instantly. He had such a friendly attitude and engaging smile. It was good to have an ally in a strange new place. Although he had tried to reassure her of his mother's kindness, Ella knew from the looks the older lady had given her that she was not someone to get on the wrong side of.

The following week was hectic. After meeting Miriam who said that she had worked the Franklins for "too many years to remember", she was constantly running here and there learning where to put this and where that was kept, who liked their meat well-done and who liked it rare, who ate breakfast at what time and everything she was expected to know to take care of the Franklins. Between the dusting, vacuuming and polishing silver, there was very little chance for her to see the Franklins except at meal times when she had to help Miriam serve. She tried her best to avoid Margaret Franklin. Despite Gregory, Jr.'s predictions, the austere lady didn't seem to warm toward her at all. In fact, she noticed that Mrs. Franklin made a point of acting as if Ella was invisible.

Mr. Franklin, Sr., however had his son's engaging smile and personality. He always asked her how she was doing and to give her mother his regards. He seemed to be quite fond of her mother and would ask about her often. Ella wondered at times if there was more than just a friendly concern for her mother. She knew that her mother had worked for the Franklins for a number of years when she was young and before she married Ella's father. She also noted that Mrs. Franklin hardly ever asked about her mother. And she would give her husband some stern glances when he inquired about her.

Mr. Franklin was a political figure of some sort and was rarely home. He traveled around the state a lot and occasionally went away on business trips to Washington, DC. On the days that both men were out of the house, Ella would feel lonely and vulnerable. Miriam was always warning her of this and that and whispering under her breath that the Missus would be angry if this or that wasn't done properly. Ella would look at the older housekeeper and vow that she would not end up acting like her for no "white" people. One day she would be married and have a nice home and not bow down to anyone.

Every night, Ella would return home, tired and sore from all of the work. She would soak her aching body in the tub, sometimes falling asleep until the cooling water woke her. Then she would have to go in the next day and start all over again. Mrs. Franklin was a relentless taskmaster. It seemed to Ella that she would think up hard chores for her to do just to show her authority. She never smiled at her or tried to engage her in any conversation. The only bright spot to the day was when Greg, Jr. would be home. He always stopped to ask her how she was doing and sometimes, he even offered her a ride home. She would accept them, but asked him to let her off on the corner. She knew that her mother would give her a severe tongue-lashing if she saw her getting out of the car with a man, especially a white man!

One night after about six months after she started to work for the Franklins, Ella was walking home when Greg Jr. pulled up beside her in his silver convertible. He asked her if she'd like a ride. He said he just had to stop at the college that he attended to pick up some material that he was working on. She had gotten finished early and Mother wasn't expecting her for another hour, so why not?

He opened the door for her and after she was in, he reached over her to fasten her seat belt. His arm brushed across her breast and she blushed. Greg, Jr. didn't seem to notice as he started the car and headed toward the college. He began talking about school and what he planned to do after college, that he wasn't interested in politics like his father. He just wanted to be an attorney. He was not interested in becoming some political bigwig like his dad. He was more interested in defending people wrongfully accused of a crime. Although, Ella did not understand everything he was talking about, she hung onto his every word. She was fascinated with this boy and she realized that she was beginning to feel an even stronger emotion for him. It frightened her, because she knew that she could not even begin to think of a serious romance with him.

When they arrived at the college, Greg went into the building for his books. She waited in the car for him, enjoying the cool summer breeze. It was a glorious evening. The setting sun colored the sky burnt orange and crickets were just beginning their nightly serenade. She saw a few lightning bugs winking their way to the lake. She sighed and closed her eyes.

"Hey," Greg's voice interrupted her. "Was I gone that long? You didn't even wake up when I opened the car door."

She blinked at him. Had she fallen asleep? They were on the highway, heading out of town. She straightened up and looked at him. "Where are we going?" She felt a momentary panic creep inside of her. Her mother would be fit to be tied if she came home late.

"I wanted to show you something. It won't take long to get there," he said without taking his eyes off of the road. She realized that the road was leading to the other side of the lake. She had been there one time with her father. He like to fish in places that were out of the way. "Fish can't stand too many people looking down at them," he'd told her. Her father was a man of few words, but he considered himself a very wise man, so most of his conversations were one saying or other.

She watched as Greg turned down a dirt road. Although she was nervous, she couldn't help but admire the scenery. The pine trees towered over them and reached out to join each other at their peaks. The setting sun winked at them through the branches. Every now and then a rabbit or squirrel made a mad dash in front of the car running to the other side of the road. Finally, Greg pulled into a dirt lane and after driving for a while longer, he came to a stop in front of a rustic cabin. Ella was awestruck with the beauty and serenity of the cabin and the forest setting surrounding it. Greg climbed out of the convertible without opening his door and came over to her side and opened the door for her. "Come on", he said. I want you to see the backside of the place." He grabbed her hand, ignoring her protests and pulled her after him to the back of the cabin.

When they reached the corner of the cabin, Ella's eyes stretched wide as she took in the beautiful scenery that stood before her. She had never envisioned that any place on earth could look like Paradise. The lawn was soft and green and it continued to follow the slope of a small hill that stopped at the edge of tall pine trees. There was a fast- running brook that separated the lawn from the hill. A flower garden arrayed in so many colors that she couldn't tell how many varieties there were ran the entire length of the house. There was a little stone footpath leading through a long arbor covered in jasmine and lilac all the way to a log-built gazebo. There were potted geraniums, poppies and ivy placed around the deck of the gazebo. There was a rustic wet bar on one side of the deck. He opened a side door of the bar, touched a button and soft music floated down from some invisible speakers overhead. He pushed another switch and floodlights lit up the surrounding area.

"It's so beautiful!" Ella whispered in awe. It's like some magic kingdom. How did you find it?"

Greg chuckled lightly, and answered, "I didn't find it. It belongs to my family. But, Mom and Dad are always too busy to spend time here, so most of the time I spend a lot of weekends here, studying or just relaxing from the hectic pace at school. Do you like it?" he asked, resembling a little boy wanting to please his mother.

"I love it!" Ella gasped. She stood up and gazed toward the hill behind the house. "I feel like running barefoot through that brook and up the hill!"

Greg sat down on the top step of the gazebo and started taking off his shoes and socks. Ella stared at him and asked, "What are you doing?" He grinned wickedly at her and jumped up, yelling behind him, "Last one up is a rotten egg!"

Ella hurried to take off her own shoes and socks, calling after him, "No fair, you had a head start!" She ran down the steps and dashed after him. She splashed through the brook ignoring the brief shock of the cold water on her feet. By the time she reached the top of the small hill, Greg was already there, on his back trying to catch his breath. She fell down beside him in a heap, gasping and laughing all at the same time. He raised himself up on one elbow and looked down at her flushed face. Her light amber eyes were sparkling and there was a tinge of pink under her golden bronze skin. He stared in amazement. He had never noticed how beautiful she was. Her long wavy black hair spread out fan-like on the grass beneath her head. Her full heart-shaped mouth glistened in the evening sunset and their softness taunted him. Her ample breasts jutted upward leading to a tiny waist and well-rounded hips. He could not stop staring at this girl-woman. He felt a strange stirring in his loins. He was not a stranger to women, but none had ever had this effect on him.

Ella was looking up at him and was having similar thoughts. His silver eyes seemed to bore into her heart and soul. His sandy-colored hair fell over his brow and hung just at the nape of his neck. There it turned into soft curls. His arms were strong and fit. His fingers were slim and manicured. She saw his eyes trace the shape of her lips and a tingling sensation started inside of her and traveled downward to hit its mark. She shivered slightly. She watched his head lower to hers and closed her eyes to receive his kiss. It was soft and searching. She returned it with joy and he felt her mouth open to receive his searching tongue. He groaned into her mouth, as he tasted the sweetness of her. She felt the tingling sensation begin to grow and she wanted to weld her body to his. She knew that this was wrong. She knew that her mother would be furious, but she could not control the fiery torment she was feeling. He began stroking her breasts through the material of her dress. She felt her nipples tighten as a strange excitement coursed through her and a fire began raging through her. He kept kissing her until she was dizzy with desire. His hands gently caressed her in places that only she had touched before. He was kissing her eyes, her neck, then her lips and her pulses began racing. She was no longer aware of time or place, just the raging fire inside of her that only he could quench. She was yearning to be loved by him and to return his love. She knew that she was losing control and that Greg was beyond the point of self-control as they both frantically began taking off each other's clothes. He kept kissing and caressing her until she was senseless with this new desire. She opened her eyes as Greg climbed above her. His lust-filled gaze met hers for an instant, as he began to enter her. She gasped at the momentary hot piercing pain, and then thrust upward as her movements matched his in the frantic dance of passion. She felt as if she were leaving her body and soaring out into space. Finally, when she could soar no higher, she heard Greg gasp and she heard a moan escape her lips as she reached the pinnacle of ecstasy. He called her name over and over as he clung tightly to her reveling in the feel and taste of her and never wanting to let her go. They were both silent as they floated back to earth. Both of them knew that this one brief encounter would not be enough. They were one. They were meant to be.

Myrtle Jones stood looking out of the window. Where in the world was Ella? She had never been this late before. She was imagining all sorts of horrible things when she saw a car stop at the end of the street. Ella emerged and she recognized the car as young Greg Franklin's when it turned the corner under a streetlight. She saw Ella hurrying toward the house. When her daughter entered the house, she looked at her flushed face and the way her daughter averted her eyes from her and she knew. *Dear God,* she silently prayed. *Please don't let history repeat itself. Don't let her fall in love and spend her life loving a Franklin. A love that can only be given secretly. A love that I've been denied all of these years and have only been able to share with myself. The love that Greg Franklin, Sr. and I shared over twenty years ago.*

The summer of nineteen forty-five was the hottest it had been in over a decade. Mama and Papa were sitting on the washed out wooden porch, fanning themselves and at the constant barrage of flies that kept landing on them. They were discussing how much cotton they had picked that day for old Mr. Franklin.

"We made $14.00 today, Ma so that should keep us in groceries and kerosene this week." Papa leaned back in his old rickety chair as if he thought that food and kerosene were all the necessities needed in life.

Myrtle looked up at him from her perch on the wooden steps and thought with disdain that Papa was such a simple man. He was satisfied eking out a living, but not her. She wanted the finer things in life. What sixteen year-old girl didn't dream of having a big house and fine husband? That's why her ears perked up at Mama's next words.

"I hear that old Mrs. Franklin is looking for a girl to work in the kitchen. I wanted to do it, but she's looking for someone a little younger."

"What about me, Mama," Myrtle interrupted. I certainly know how to clean." She was referring to the never-ending chore of trying to keep the run-down shack they lived in clean and fresh smelling. She had spent many hours on her hands and knees scrubbing the wooden floors until they were almost white from the lye soap and bleach that she used.

Mama threw a worried glance in Papa's direction. "I don't

know, it's such a big house and a lot of work. And old Mrs. Franklin is a mean thing to work for I hear."

Myrtle straightened her back and tossed her head in that stubborn way that she had when she was determined to get her way and said, "I'm not afraid of no Mrs. Franklin. I'll just go about my business and do such a good job that she won't never have to be saying anything to me."

Papa smiled at Mama behind his daughter's back. He rarely had a harsh word to say to Myrtle as she was a 'daddy's girl' and he could never refuse her anything. He said to Mama, "I don't see no reason why the girl can't give it a try. Lord knows we could use the extra money around here. I'll go and talk to old Mrs. Franklin, tomorrow."

Myrtle jumped up and hugged Papa around the neck and said, "Oh, thank you, Papa. I promise to do a good job and try to help you out around here." But, she also knew that she was going to sneak a little bit of money at a time out of her earnings and save it to buy some lace hankies and perfume and other little trinkets that she had seen on the snooty white girls when she went to town. She knew that she was prettier than a lot of them. Her skin was the color of caramel and her eyes were slanted with long lashes that swept upward. Her cheekbones did not deny the Indian heritage that she boasted. Her mother's family had come from Louisiana somewhere and she was rich in Creole blood. Her thick, wavy black hair hung to the center of her back and she would use pomade on it and brush it every night until it gleamed. She was petite with shapely legs and tapered ankles. All of the local boys vied for her attention, but she ignored them. She was looking for someone much more than a cotton-picker's son. She wanted wealth and status. So, eventually the boys stopped trying to win her over labeling her stuck up and ' thinking she was better than everyone'.

The next day Papa came home with good news. old Mrs. Franklin wanted her to start the next day. Myrtle was so excited. She went to her room at the far end of the house to see what she could wear the next day. Actually her room was in the corner of the one bedroom, where her parent's slept. She had a curtain hung to give them all some privacy. She pulled the box from under the cot that she slept on and opened it. Inside it were the few 'nice' clothes that she had. She pulled out a plaid pleated skirt and a white blouse. She looked for the one pair of stockings that she owned and laid them on top of the other articles. Then she looked under the bed and pulled out a box containing her good Sunday shoes. *There*, she thought. *Tonight I'll heat up some water and take a bath and wash my hair. I need to make a good first impression. I know I will,* she thought smugly.

When she arrived with Papa at the big white house with the huge double-doors, she felt a little frightened. She felt like she had on her first day in school when Papa had left her at the front door and she had to walk into that roomful of strangers. She had been brave all the while that Papa was with her, but now she would be on her own and she had never been on her own for a long time.

Papa rapped three times on the door with the large bronze knocker. A stooped man in a butler's uniform opened the door after about five minutes of them waiting and ushered them inside. He told them to wait in the study over there and he would go get the 'Missus'.

They entered the large, airy room and Myrtle sat gingerly on the curved sofa while Papa stood next to it, seeming out of place in the gold and white room. The furniture was very ornate, with its white velvet furniture and delicate tables where vases of freshly cut flowers sat. There was a grand piano in the corner of the room and a huge desk at the opposite end. It was covered with papers and didn't look as if it ever got straightened.

Myrtle's heart pounded with excitement as she looked at this beautiful room. *Oh, to live like this*, she thought. She imagined herself sitting at the piano in a filmy, flowing dress as her husband stood over her to grant her every wish. She was so deep in her reverie that she did not hear the door opening and did not know that old Mrs. Franklin had entered until she heard her clear her throat.

She snapped her head around to stare directly into the grayest eyes that she'd ever seen. The woman's hair was almost the same color as her eyes. Her face belied her age as the skin was smooth and her features were aristocratic. She would have been beautiful, but she never smiled. She just continued to stare at Myrtle causing her to become quite uncomfortable under the scrutiny.

" So, you're the girl who wants to work for me? I hope your Papa told you that I'm not a person with patience for laziness or half-done work. I like a spotless kitchen and that's all I will accept from you, do you understand?'
Her eyes seemed to bore right to the core of Myrtle.

Myrtle had lost her voice and her bravery under the glare of the lady's crystal eyes so all she could do was nod and edge closer to Papa. She began to wonder if this had been such a good idea.

"What's the matter with you, girl? Cat got your tongue? I want you to answer me when I speak to you, not stand there like you're retarded, do you hear?" Her voice rose as she spoke

Myrtle found her voice albeit it was squeaky when she answered. "Yes Ma'am." She had never been so frightened in her life.

Papa cleared his throat and said, "She's just a little nervous, ma'am. But, she is a good worker and a fine girl. I know she will do you proud, ma'am." He was twirling his hat nervously and looking around the room at everything but old Mrs. Franklin.

"Well, she'd better do a good job, or she'll be out of here faster than greased lightning!" With that said, the lady got up and told them to follow her to the kitchen where Myrtle would meet the cook and the gardener. She explained to them that anything that the cook assigned her to do would be her duty. "Things change around here constantly. Our son Gregory is finishing his last semester at law school and will be getting married next summer so we will be doing a lot of preparation for that since the wedding will be held here."

As they approached the door to the kitchen, the front door burst open and a tall boy galloped in followed by a giggling blonde girl about the same age. They both had on tennis outfits and her white pleated skirt was so short that Myrtle could see the little white shorts underneath. They were smiling at each other and she was looking up at him and coyly batting her eyelashes at him.

They finally noticed the three of them standing in the hallway and the tall boy grinned at them with the biggest smile and whitest teeth that Myrtle had ever seen. He walked briskly up to his mother and gave her a kiss on the cheek. For the first time since their arrival, Myrtle saw the lady smile. Her smile was as brilliant as her son's and you could see that she adored him and he adored her. Then the boy looked at Myrtle and her father. "Hey there, Smitty." Myrtle guessed that was the name they referred to her father as when he was at work. She personally found it to be quite distasteful coming from someone young enough to be Papa's son and she did not try to hide the feeling that must have shown on her face, because she saw the tall boy look at her with the same gray eyes that his mother had and she saw the flicker of amusement in them. "And who might this be?" he asked.

His mother explained that she was the new 'hired help' and would be working in the kitchen. She winced at the way his mother said 'hired help' as if it were a disease. The tall boy noticed Myrtle's discomfort and the proud way she held her head and his voice softened as he looked down at her. "Well, welcome aboard, little one. We'll try not to make it too hard on you around here." He smiled at her and Myrtle felt a strange feeling inside of her stomach as she looked up into his gray eyes. The girl in the short skirt saw the look that passed between them and after giving Myrtle a hateful glare, she slithered up to the boy who had been called Gregory and pouted at him. "Come on, Greg, you promised me a bowl of vanilla ice cream if I won

LA JUANDA HUFF BISHOP

the match." She was pulling his arm and after smiling at them all again, he let himself be led into the sitting room by the pushy girl. The special look that had passed between Myrtle and her son had not gone unnoticed by old Mrs. Franklin either, because her tone became suddenly more impatient and rude as she snapped at Myrtle. "Hurry up! Don't dawdle. I want you to get to work!'

Myrtle reluctantly brought her attention back to the lady, but her thoughts stayed on the very handsome boy with the wonderful smile. He was as handsome as a movie star. *Maybe it won't be so bad working here after all,* she thought. So with her head held high and a secret smile on her face, she followed the lady into the kitchen.

CHAPTER EIGHT

"Mama?" Lively repeated, seeing her mother's flushed face and unseeing eyes. "Mama, I asked you twice if you are all right?" Ella's head lifted suddenly and she looked around the room as if she had never seen it before. Lively wondered what her mother could have been daydreaming about that had taken her so long to respond.

Mama looked at her daughter and smiled. "I guess I was just thinking too hard," she hedged. Lively knew that it was more than that, but did not press her mother with any more questions. Somehow she knew that she would not get any answers from her. She wished Mama would talk to her. She needed to ask her what these strange emotions were that she herself was feeling. Last night, she had tossed and turned for several hours before falling into a fitful sleep. A sleep laced with dreams of kisses, tingling sensations in her private area and a smiling face poised over hers. But, she didn't know how to approach the subject. Mama and Grandma always seemed a little distant whenever the subject of boys came up. So, Lively changed the subject.

"Mama, I've got my room all cleaned and all of my homework is done. I was wondering if I could go over to Janelle's for a while. We're working on a special project for science class," she lied. She really hated lying to Mama, but she didn't want her to know that the sole purpose of a visit with her friend was to talk about the dance and the kiss afterwards.

"Well, Grandma and I are going to Sunday night worship service and we were hoping that you'd go with us," Mama answered.

Lively thought quickly and said, "I'd love to Mama, but this project has to be done by Wednesday. That only gives us two days to get it ready," she finished, hoping that the wide-eyed innocent look she gave Mama was convincing enough. She knew how important school and good grades were to Mama.

"Okay, just this once. You know that Grandma expects you to go with us to church at least twice a month and you have only been with us one time this month," Mama scolded, but she relented and allowed her to go. "Just be home at eight. Tomorrow is a school day, and I've got to leave early for work. Greg Franklin, Jr. will be arriving tomorrow afternoon and Mrs. Franklin has a special meal she wants me to prepare." Mama felt a flutter in her chest. She would be seeing Greg, tomorrow. She had not seen him since that awful day, sixteen years ago.

Ella sat on the tattered sofa in the small living room facing her mother and father. Her mother was crying and refusing to look at her. Her father was pacing the floor like an angry bull, occasionally halting his steps to yell an expletive her way.

"We are hard-working Christian people!" he yelled. "How could you go and do something like this to us. We taught you right from wrong and look at you! We helped you get a good job and like a tramp, you go and lay with your employer's son.

How could you do this to your mother and ME?" He seemed to make a threatening move toward her. Ella cringed from him, as her mother laid a restraining hand on his arm.

"Don't Edmund," she pleaded through her tears. Her father looked at her mother for a few seconds, as he went to stand by the old wood stove, staring unseeingly at the flames through the grilled panel on the front of the stove. For a while the crackling of the fire was the only sound in the room. Then her father turned to her.

"You know that you've got yourself in a mess!" He looked at her as if he didn't remember that she was his daughter. "There's no way that Margaret Franklin is going to let her son marry you! They probably won't even claim the child as their grandchild. Your mother and I can't afford another mouth to feed. So, you better be thinking up some answers, girl!" He cursed again and slammed out of the room. The room was silent except for an occasional sniffle from her mother who would still not look at her. Ella felt so isolated. She wanted to explain to her mother that she was not a tramp. That she loved Greg and he loved her. What they had shared was not dirty, but warm and wonderful. They had often discussed the probability of marriage. Each of them knew that there would be a lot of obstacles to face. Interracial marriages were rarely heard of in their state and non-existent in this town. She knew the embarrassment it would cause his family if the news of their relationship got around. She knew that they had high hopes for their only son and his mother would never allow him to marry her. When she had told Greg that she was pregnant, he was more concerned for her than for himself. He told her that he loved her and that he would stand by her, no matter what. They both knew that it would be hard, but they wanted to be together. Greg wanted to find a good job and move away with her to a more accepting city.

Ella wanted to say all of this to her mother, but she could tell by the rigid set to her shoulders that it would be useless to try to make her understand. All she could do was sit quietly with her head down in shame until she was allowed to escape to the privacy of her little room . The only hope that sustained her was in knowing that Greg was facing his parents right now with the same news.

"What are you telling us, son?" His father's gray eyes, so like his own stared at him. His mother sat in the Queen Anne chair holding a lacy handkerchief to her eyes, wailing dramatically. He took a deep breath and continued. "I said that Ella is pregnant. It is my child and I love her and want to marry her. I was hoping that you would give us your blessing and support us financially until I can find a job somewhere.

The silence in the study was like a thick blanket. His mother continued her wailing into her handkerchief and his father kept looking at anything but him. Finally he asked, "What about your scholarship to the University? You can't be thinking about giving that up! You've already been accepted!"

Greg, Jr. did not waver. "I know Dad. I've thought about that, too. I wish I could go, but I've got to think about Ella and the baby. I need to own up to my responsibility. And contrary to what you may think, Mom, Ella is a sweet, kind and innocent girl. It was as much my fault as it was hers. Besides, I love her. I want to marry her," he finished.

His mother lowered the handkerchief from her face and looked at her son. She saw the gleam of determination and defiance in his eyes. She felt raw anger bubbling to the surface as she thought about that girl lying naked with her son. She knew not to repeat the word to Greg, but it echoed over and over in her mind. *Slut, slut, SLUT!*

His father cleared his throat, sat down in the large winged-back chair by the fireplace and placed his head in his hands. After a few moments, he looked up and said, "Well, this is certainly a shock. Everything has changed so quickly. You must give us time to think about this. You're supposed to be leaving for school in two months and now this. Your mother and I need to talk about this turn of events. Leave us alone for a while," his father said walking to the doorway with his son. Greg, Jr. left the room and Greg, Sr. turned to his wife, who was loudly blowing her nose and looking at him through red-rimmed eyes.

"What are we going to do?" she cried out in an anguished voice. "How can we face our family and friends?" Her husband gave her a look of reproach as he came to stand beside her chair.

"Now, dear, we don't need to be worrying about that yet. Our main concern right now is our son and his future. And also the welfare of our grandchild." He saw his wife flinch at the mention of the baby as her grandchild, and he continued. "And whether you want to accept the fact or not, the child is our grandchild."

He watched as his wife pondered that fact for some minutes.

He waited for her to look at him again before saying, "I have thought of a solution that just might satisfy everyone. A solution where Greg can go on to school this fall, and Ella and the child will be taken care of. We need to call the girl and her parents and invite them over to discuss my plan," he concluded, looking very calm and self-assured. He was well known in the political circle for settling issues quickly and with the least amount of publicity. He had been a powerful attorney, whose court cases resembled strategic battles in which he was almost always the victor.

CHAPTER NINE

Ella sat in the old truck between her mother and father. The silence was overwhelming and she sunk low in the seat wishing she could disappear. She was afraid. She did not want to face Greg's parents. She had never been comfortable around Mrs. Franklin and always kept out of her way. She knew that the old lady did not like her and wondered what type of reception she was going to get now. She looked out of the corner of her eye at her father. His face was like granite. He was concentrating very hard on the road and she could feel the anger coming from him like a raging fire. She looked at her mother out of the other eye and her face was an exact replica of her father's. She had never felt so ashamed or so alone.

There were other thoughts going through Myrtle's mind as she sat in the truck looking out of the window and watching the scenery passing by. What would it be like sitting in Greg, Sr.'s home after all of these years? She remembered the last time that she had been there. It was a memory that would be forever ingrained in her mind.

"How dare you come into my home and do something like this to us?" old Mrs. Franklin was leaning forward in her chair as she glared at Myrtle with as much vengeance as she could muster. "You knew when you met my son that he was engaged to Clara, yet you allowed this to happen. And then you continued this filthy liaison even after he and Clara married! How could you?" Greg, and his wife Clara were sitting in the room while his mother berated Myrtle. He wouldn't look at her even though her eyes beseeched him to. She felt so alone in the room with just Papa. Mama had gotten ill last winter and the infection had spread through her frail body so rapidly that she did not even have a chance at survival.

Clara was sitting in a winged-back chair with a handkerchief held to her reddened eyes and mewing pitifully. Greg had his arm along the back of the chair and was trying to soothe her. Myrtle could see that she was very far along in her pregnancy while she was just in her third month.

Old Professor Franklin stood off to the side by the fireplace and said nothing. Myrtle could see that he was very uncomfortable with the situation and let his wife do all of the talking.

Myrtle felt herself getting angry, not only with Greg's mother, but also at Greg. How dare he sit there and not come to her defense? He, who had pursued her until she had given in. He had participated in this affair as much as she had and now that she was pregnant and his family had found out, he was going to sit there as if she didn't exist. How dare he? She squared her shoulders and held her head high and said haughtily to old Mrs. Franklin.

"Begging your pardon, ma'am, but Greg was involved in this as much as I was. I had no intention of interfering in his life or relationship. I merely came here to work. I am not a tramp. I loved your son. And I realize now that it was wrong. But, there is *my* child to consider in this." She looked at Clara

Franklin when she said this.

Old Mrs. Franklin looked at her as if she had taken leave of her senses. "What do you mean!?" she demanded. "Surely you don't think that you can have that baby. It would ruin our name and good-standing in this state."

Suddenly, Clara Franklin stopped wailing long enough to look at her husband and demand that he never have anything to do with "that trollop" again and that he do something about "that bastard" that she was carrying. If he didn't abide by this, she would tell everybody all over town what he and that woman had done. Then she put the handkerchief back up to her eyes and continued wailing.

So in the end it was decided that the best for all concerned was to get rid of the baby, let Myrtle go and never have contact again. Myrtle was heartbroken. She had loved Greg Franklin for four years. How could he just throw away their love like that? She remembered the nights that she had secretly lain in his arms and they had talked about everything. She knew that there could never be a future for them, but she was just content to love and be loved by him. She also knew that he did not love Clara. He thought her to be a spoiled, selfish and over-indulged young lady, but she came from an affluent family and his mother felt that she would be the perfect match for her son. So, Myrtle went home with Papa, where she stayed and cared for him for the next two years until he died. She then met her husband and they married and the pain subsided. But to this day, she knew that she still loved Greg Franklin, Sr.. And now it had all come back to haunt her.

When they pulled up in front of the white house, Ella had a sudden urge to leap from the cab and start running as fast as she could in the other direction. Her father must have sensed this and said roughly, "Come on, let's get this over with." They climbed the steps to the door with Ella hanging back, reluctantly. She had a trapped look in her eyes as she climbed the steps with leaden feet. Her father pounded the heavy knocker four times and they waited silently. Miriam opened the door and silently led them to the study. She knocked on the door and then quickly scurried away before anyone answered.

Mr. Franklin opened the door, giving them a reserved smile and invited them into the room. There was a fire burning brightly in the fireplace, but a chill enveloped the room. Her father stood just inside of the door with his hat in his hands. Her mother stood beside him, a rebellious look in her eyes as she looked at Mrs. Franklin. But, Ella saw a different look in her eyes as she looked at Mr. Franklin. An almost tender, loving look and the hard lines in her face softened. The same look came into Mr. Franklin's eyes, fleetingly, and then he regained his composure and became very business-like in his manner. Ella saw her mother's face harden again. Mrs. Franklin was looking at Myrtle with venom in her gaze, and didn't acknowledge her with any formalities. Ella knew that the two women were silently locked in some long-ago battle, but she couldn't dwell on it right now.

Greg, Jr. sat in a chair opposite his mother. He threw Ella a warm look and smiled at her. She saw the love shining in his eyes as he looked at her. Mr. Franklin waved them into the room and asked them to sit in the three chairs reserved for them. Everyone was silent for a few moments, then, Mr. Franklin cleared his throat and began to speak.

74

"I suppose there is no reason for preliminaries. We all know why we're here. We have a problem and we need to find a solution that will benefit everyone," his glance encompassed each person in the room and seemed to linger on Myrtle a split second longer than anyone else..

"Mr. And Mrs. Jones,' he continued. "It was just brought to our attention this afternoon that your daughter is expecting and our son is the baby's father." No one in the room saw the hateful glance that Mrs. Franklin threw her way, except Ella. She dropped her eyes and did not look up until Mr. Franklin began to speak, again. "Mrs. Franklin and I discussed this situation this afternoon and wanted to share our suggestion with you. As you know, our son has a bright future ahead of him. He has already been accepted to attend the State University on an academic scholarship. He is to leave for school in two months. Neither he nor your daughter will even consider the idea of terminating the pregnancy, so here is what we decided." Everyone in the room was leaning forward and listening attentively to him. "We thought that Ella could continue to work for us until her she can no longer work due to the advanced state of her pregnancy. We would be responsible for all of her medical bills to include delivery and hospital stay when the baby is born. We will also increase her salary so that it would not put a burden on you when the child is born. We will purchase all the necessary items for the baby and provide it with whatever it needs. Greg, Jr. can then go to school to finish his education and once he is finished, if he and Ella still feel that they have a future together, then, he will be in a much better position to provide for a wife and child. But, there is one stipulation to this agreement." He looked around the room at all of them.

They waited to hear what he was going to say next.

"Because of my position in this state, my reputation and my family's reputation must be nearly impeccable. It is of the utmost importance that no one ever finds about this until I am no longer involved in any political activities and Greg, Jr. and Ella are of legal age. It is imperative that this be kept as quiet as possible." When he finished speaking, he sat down in the winged-back chair and waited for his proposal to sink in.

Ella's father sat twirling his hat in his hands, looking first at her, then at her mother. Finally, he spoke. "Well, Mr. Franklin, I know that we both have our family's best interests at heart and even though I know we can't afford another mouth to feed, I am a Christian man. I would never allow my daughter to take away an innocent life. I also believe that however you make your bed, hard or soft, you have to lay in it. Your concern for your son's schooling and your family's reputation and your standing in this state are understandable, too. So, speaking on behalf of my family, I appreciate your generous offer and we will accept it." He stood to shake Mr. Franklin's hand in agreement, and then said, "Now, if you'll excuse us, we need to be heading home. Ella will be here tomorrow morning to work at her usual time." He tipped his hat to Mrs. Franklin. "Evenin,' ma'am," he said and headed toward the door.

Ella stood to follow and cast a glance toward Greg's mother. She sat in her chair wearing a smug smile of victory. She dared to look at Greg, Jr. and he mouthed, "Meet me at the corner, tomorrow" to her. In her heart she knew that it would be the last meeting for them.

She did not know that Mrs. Franklin was thinking the same thing. She vowed to herself that her son would never marry her if she had anything to say about it. She would be the victor as she had been before.

The next evening Ella hurried toward the corner to meet Greg. She looked at her watch and noticed that she was a few minutes early, so she sat down on the grass under a willow tree to wait for him. She was thinking of what a wonderful life they would have together. Their child would be shown all of the love that she had been denied growing up. She felt tears well up in her eyes as she thought of all the times that she had longed for her mother and father to hug her and show her some affection.

She was so deep in her thoughts that she had lost track of the time. It was already eight o'clock. Greg had not come yet and she knew that she had better get home. Mama and Papa would be very angry. With tears streaming down her face, she hurried home. She didn't know that only five minutes after she left, Greg had come hurrying to the corner to meet her. He had tried to be there on time, but his mother had suddenly gotten one of her fainting spells when he was getting ready to leave and detained him longer than he had expected. When he finally was able to leave, he was oblivious to the smug look of satisfaction on his mother's face.

CHAPTER TEN

Lively hurried to her friend's house. She couldn't wait to see Janelle and talk about all the exciting events from last night. She especially wanted to talk about her first kiss. Her pulses raced as she remembered the taste and feel of Randy's lips on hers.

She was so preoccupied with her thoughts as she passed old Mr. Pete's store that she did not see the hateful gaze of Curtis Sampson on her as she hurried on her way. He was standing just inside of the open doorway swallowing the last drops of his Pepsi as he watched her and would have followed her if old Mr. Pete hadn't interrupted him by asking him about his father. Still, his feverish eyes followed her to the corner. She turned toward the area that was dubbed High Town by the people from this side of town. He knew that her friend Janelle lived there. But, he was more concerned with someone else who lived there. That same someone he had seen with his filthy lips and hands on Lively last night. He felt a burning rage surge through him. He had been obsessed with Lively since grade school. She had been such a pretty little girl with her long black braids and starched dresses. She would always swing with him at recess and sometimes at lunchtime, she would share her sandwich with him. That meant that she loved him, too, didn't it? His bulging eyes were feverish with frustration and he vowed to get revenge on the man who had taken away the love of his life.

As Lively continued toward Janelle's house, she heard a car pull up alongside her. She didn't recognize the car so she quickened her step. Then, she heard a familiar voice call out, "Hey, Lady Dimples, what's your hurry?" She turned and saw Randy's smiling face. She stopped and smiled at him.

He got out of his car and came around to the passenger side, "If you're in that big of a hurry, then let me get you there even faster," he said opening the door for her. She hesitated only for a second and got in. He got back into the driver's seat and asked her where she was headed. She told him that she was on her way to Janelle's house and after giving him directions, she fell silent, suddenly feeling very shy, thinking of the kiss they had shared the previous night.

Randy did not seem to notice her reticence and carried on a friendly banter all the way to Janelle's. When they pulled up in front of her house, he turned the engine off and turned to look at her. He looked at her mouth as if he were going to kiss her again. She could fill goose bumps rising along her arms in anticipation. Instead of kissing her, he began to speak in a soft voice. "You know, after I left you last night, I went back to the party and the joy had gone out of the evening for me. I don't know what it is about you, but I know that I enjoyed last night with you more than I've ever enjoyed with anyone. You're beautiful and mysterious and shy all at the same time. I wish you were sixteen already, so we could see more of each other. I hope that I'm not being to forward, but you intrigue me, Lady Dimples." He leaned over and kissed her lightly on the lips, then got out and opened her door for her. He smiled and winked at her as he got back into the car and drove off down the street.

She watched until the car turned the corner out of sight. She floated up the steps and into Janelle's house.

Lively laughed excitedly to herself as she stretched languidly in her bed. She looked toward the window and saw the sun streaming through the filmy curtains. What a glorious day! It was her birthday! She was finally sixteen. She looked at the chair in the corner of the bedroom and saw her birthday presents from Mama and Grandma.

She could hardly wait until this afternoon to wear the new white Capri-style pants and lime colored halter. She even had a brand-new pair of white sandals and they had given her gold hoop earring and a gold bracelet. She would be going to the movies with Janelle and she knew that her friend had invited Randy to meet them there, even though it was supposed to be a surprise.

This was going to be the best birthday ever. She got up, put on her robe and house slippers and after going to the bathroom to splash cold water on her face, she ran to the kitchen. As usual Mama was already there, but today Grandma was there, too. They started singing "Happy Birthday" as soon as she entered the room. Mama had a big pile of pancakes steaming on the table. Grandma was bustling to and from the table with milk, coffee, margarine and whatever else Mama had not gotten around to doing yet. The mood in the kitchen this morning was festive, but Lively thought Mama was even more jovial than usual. She kept telling jokes and giggling like a schoolgirl. Her eyes were sparkling and she looked very pretty. Lively noticed that she also wore a hint of eye shadow and lipstick. What was going on? Mama never wore makeup to work. Lively saw

Grandma staring at Mama with a slightly puzzled frown on her face, too.

But, pretty soon they were all caught up in the festive mood of the day. Mama said that she would be working later tonight, but they would have her birthday cake and ice cream when she got home. Lively promised to be home from the movies early so that she could celebrate her birthday with them, too.

The weather outside promised to be a warm, sunny day. It seemed as though Mother Nature had ordered the weather just for her birthday. The leaves on the trees were a bright green. She could hear meadowlarks singing in their branches. She stood on the porch in her robe and breathed the air laced with jasmine and honeysuckle. She looked up and down the almost deserted road. Then she saw him. Curtis Sampson was standing on the corner staring in her direction. He turned abruptly when he realized he had been seen and quickly walked away. For some reason Lively felt a strange uneasiness at seeing him. There was something menacing in his attitude lately. She couldn't understand it because she had known Curtis all of her life, practically. But, whatever, she knew that she would definitely need to start being careful whenever she was anywhere around him.

CHAPTER ELEVEN

When Lively arrived at the downtown theater, Janelle, Randy and the boy that Janelle had met at the dance were already there, waiting for her. As she got near enough to hear them, they shouted in unison, "Happy Birthday Lively!" Other moviegoers turned to smile at her as she approached the trio. She felt her face flush and not just from all the attention. Randy had a single red rose in a crystal vase and he leaned over and kissed her on the cheek, murmuring, "Happy birthday, sweet sixteen and never been kissed." His eyes twinkled in merriment and she couldn't help but laugh out loud at the double meaning of his birthday wish.

They all went inside and found seats. Randy had bought popcorn and sodas for everyone and they all settled comfortably in their seats and began to watch the movie. It was a comedy and very funny. They laughed until their sides hurt. During the movie, Randy held Lively's hand and occasionally she would see him staring at her. She knew that she looked especially nice today. The Capri pants fit snugly on her ample hips. The lime-green top defined the rounded curve of her breasts. Since she was now sixteen, Mama had allowed her to be more liberal in applying her make-up and had even helped her with it. She had on light green eye shadow, mascara and a gold-colored lipstick. She did not apply any blush to her cheeks because with her light complexion, there was already some pink undertone in her cheeks.

When the movie was over, they all went to Hoppy's, a favorite hangout of the kids in High Town. Lively ordered a hamburger plate, while Randy ordered a chicken sandwich plate. They ate heartily and when they were finished, Randy leaned over and whispered something to Janelle. Janelle nodded and left the table. Randy turned back to her with a mischievous look in his eye. Then Lively heard a commotion behind her and turned to see all of Hoppy's staff standing there holding a birthday cake with sixteen lighted candles. When they saw her look in their direction, they burst loudly into "*Happy birthday to you!*" Lively looked at Randy with an 'I'm-going-to-get-you-for-this-look' After finishing the song, the staff brought the cake birthday plates and ice cream to their table, wished Lively a happy sixteenth birthday and went back to their duties.

Janelle had dissolved in a fit of laughter. "You should have seen your face! You turned positively beet-red. I can't wait to see the birthday picture that the staff took while they were singing happy birthday. There will be three humans and a tomato sitting at our table." They all laughed good-naturedly at her comparison, ate cake and ice cream until Lively thought she would explode. When someone looked at their watch and saw that it was nine o'clock, Lively reluctantly said that she needed to get home. Her mother would be getting home at nine-thirty and she wanted to celebrate some of her birthday with them before Grandma went to bed.

Janelle and Lively went outside to wait for the two boys to pay the bill. Janelle hugged her saying. "You know that Randy is crazy about you, girl! He planned this whole party for you. I think he's going to ask you to be his lady."

Lively gave her a questioning look. "But, what about Terri Ann," she wanted to know. She had thought that he and the cheerleader were going steady.

Janelle patted her hand and remarked, "That ended the night of the dance. When Randy returned from walking you home, Terri Ann was livid. She started yelling and calling him names. He finally had to take her home and called off the relationship that night, so I hear. So, the ball's in your court now." She finished with a conspiratorial wink at Lively. Just then, Randy and Janelle's date came out of the restaurant. Janelle and Lively hugged each other. Janelle promised to call her the next day and she and her date walked toward his car.

Randy offered her his arm and together they began walking. He turned her to him and gave her a long kiss. She wrapped her arms around his neck as the kiss deepened. Abruptly Randy pulled away and gave her a searching look. She saw his features soften as he spoke. "I really care a lot for you Lively. I think I'm falling in love with you. I don't know how you feel about me, but I hope you like me a little bit." He smiled down at her as he said this.

Like him! She had been in love with him for two years! She looked up at him and said, "Oh, Randy, I would love to go out with you. I-I- think I love you, too." She felt breathless as she finished. They kissed again, and started walking toward her house. Lively felt so light-hearted and happy. They held hands and laughed and talked about everything. He told her of his plans to become a civil rights attorney. He wanted to fight for clients who were low income and could not afford good legal assistance. She told him about her dream of becoming a Fashion Merchandiser for a large chain of department stores. She wanted to travel around the country buying and consulting with other big names in the fashion industry. This had been her dream since she was a child sitting in her room looking at the pictures in fashion magazines.

She felt suddenly shy, thinking that Randy might think her dream childish, but he seemed to be genuinely interested in what she was saying, encouraging her to follow her dream. He said, "You can be anything that you want to be as long as you have the desire, the courage and faith in yourself. The world needs all kinds of people knowing all kinds of things. I think that the fashion industry will be a better place with you in it."

As he finished talking, they turned onto her street. They were so engrossed in conversation, in each other's presence and being newly in love that they did not notice the shadowy figure lurking in the dark outside of old Mr. Pete's store. He was watching the couple laughing and holding hands and he felt a burning rage start deep inside of his brain. How could she do this to him? He had loved her for so long. He had lain in bed many nights with the image of her naked body in his head as he feverishly relieved himself from the searing flames in his loins. He would muffle the moaning that escaped his lips by placing the pillow over his head. He could not let his father hear any sound coming from his room after dark. He knew that his drunken father would beat him with anything he could find if he was awakened from his alcohol induced sleep.

Now, standing in the shadows, Curtis Sampson vowed that tonight he had to have her before HE took her away from him. He had to make her realize that she really was in love with him and not that Randy Simmons. And if he couldn't make her realize it, then he would make her pay.

CHAPTER TWELVE

The full moon was sailing slowly across the night sky and a soft breeze cooled Lively's feverish skin as Randy stood with her beneath the sycamore tree and began kissing her slowly and sensuously. It was a kiss that held a promise of love and passion in the future. She sighed softly and snuggled into his embrace and enjoyed the new beginning of love. She had only read about these moments in the romance novels that she kept hidden in her closet. Sometimes, at night, when she couldn't sleep and the house was nice and quiet, she would turn on her bedside lamp and engulf herself in the romance and intrigue of renegade lovers and fair maidens. She used to imagine herself the heroine in these daring tales of lust and adventure.

Tonight was real, though. The captain of the football team, the senior class president and the most popular and handsome boy in school was kissing her. And best of all, he liked her. When the kiss ended, he held her for a while longer then said that he'd better get going, so that she could go in and finish celebrating her birthday with her family. She thanked him again for a wonderful day. He promised to call her the next day and started walking away. That was when she remembered that she had left her vase with the rose in it at Hoppy's. She started to call out to him, but decided against it. She was sure that the staff at Hoppy's would keep it for her and she would go and get it tomorrow. She watched Randy walk to the end of the street, turn right and then he was out of sight. She turned toward the house and started up the steps, when she thought she heard a slight sound behind her. Before she could turn around to see where the sound came from, a hand covered her mouth and strong arms grabbed her and started pulling her toward the tall Johnson grass in the field away from her house. She was frozen in fear as she struggled uselessly to free herself from her captor's grip.

She wanted to scream, but the hand that covered her mouth prevented any sound from escaping. The hand was course and had a putrid smell about it that made her gag and she felt vomit rising in her throat. Finally when they reached the middle of the field, her unknown assailant softened his grip somewhat.

She was spun around and looked into the face of Curtis Sampson. He was breathing hard and his breath was so rancid that she had to turn her face away or she knew the vomit she had squelched before would not be held back this time. Then Curtis began to speak, his voice ragged and evil sounding.

"I didn't mean to scare you, Lively, but I seen you with that Randy Simmons. You know you been my girlfriend since we was in school. What you doing with him?" She looked at Curtis and what she saw in his eyes in the moonlight frightened her, and she knew that she was truly with a madman. With every word he spoke, he gripped her arm until she cried out in pain. He slapped her and told her to keep quiet. Her head snapped sideways with the force of the blow and she stumbled to the ground. She looked up and he was looming over her. He was still talking and she noticed that he seemed to be talking more about someone else than her. "All my life, you been beating me and calling me names. I still loved you. Now I seen you with him, with his hands all over you and kissing you. Bitch! Since you been throwing your body to every Tom, Dick and Harry, I'm going to get my share. You're a whore, just like my mama." He reached down and yanked her from the ground. He started kissing her roughly, slobbering into her mouth. He had a tight grip on her hair as he pulled her head back to meet his lips. She started gagging fiercely and his hands tightened their grip. She moaned in pain. He released her mouth and at the same instant she saw his fist coming at her face. The blow stunned her and she felt something warm trickling from her mouth. He pushed her to the ground and started pounding her in her face, stomach and chest. All the while he was ranting like a wild man. Sometimes his words were unintelligible moaning, sounding like a wounded animal. She tried to call out for help, but her mouth was too swollen and painful so only a pitiful mewing sound escaped her lips. She tried to turn her body away from the endless pounding that she was taking, but to no avail. Curtis just kept rolling her back toward him and his incessant punching and cursing.

When he finally had exhausted himself with beating her, he knew that he had to silence her for good so that his father wouldn't find out what he'd done. He reached inside of his coat and pulled out a small hunting knife. Lively turned her head slightly to look at her captor in the ensuing silence. In the moonlight, she saw the glint of something his hand. She instantly knew that it was a knife and that he intended to use it on her. She tried to summon some strength from within to save herself, but she was too weak. As Curtis raised the knife she tried to roll away from it and felt it pierce her side. She gagged on the scream that was in her throat because her mouth was full of blood and dirt and she felt the burning pain rip through her body. As he raised his hand again, she felt him being forcefully being pulled from her. Through the increasing fog that rolled over her eyes she saw Randy with Curtis in his large handed grip his feet dangling off the ground. Randy raised his fist and she heard a loud thud against Curtis' face, before a merciful blackness pulled her away from the agonizing pain.

Lively thought she was dreaming about Mama and Grandma sitting in her room, talking to her while she tried to sleep. She tried to open her eyes to see what they were doing there and she tried to tell them to please be quiet, because she was so sleepy. She hated being this sleepy. She could hear people talking and coming and going, but she just couldn't seem to wake up. She kept drifting back into the black void that seemed to keep pulling her away from the voices and the light.

Finally, the darkness began to recede and she pulled her heavy lids open. At first, she only saw a blur of colors. Then the colors began to take shape. She turned her head slightly toward the light and saw Mama sitting in a chair. It was by the window. She turned her head toward the other side of the room and was frightened by its unfamiliarity. Where was she? She tried to ask, and must have made some slight sound, because Mama was instantly by the side of the bed. She grabbed her hand and kissed it and started crying and kissing her on her forehead. What was going on? Then her mother looked at the other side of the room and exclaimed, "Oh Greg, she's awake! She's going to make it. Our little girl is going to be all right!"

Lively watched as a tall distinguished-looking white man came to stand by her mother's side. He placed his arm around her shoulder possessively. Lively was so confused. Who was

LIVELY

this man hugging her mother? He was a very handsome man in his late thirties or early forties. He had sandy-colored hair with a few sprinkles of gray in it. But, it was his eyes that Lively noticed, even in her drugged state. They were such a light silver color that they were almost transparent. Lively wanted to ask her mother who he was, but once again the darkness claimed her and her questions would have to wait.

It was late evening when Lively woke up again. She could see the red glow of the setting sun through the window and felt a slight breeze blowing in across the room and her face. She looked toward the hallway and saw nurses hurrying in and out of patient rooms, carrying charts or medications or answering call lights. She felt so alone and bewildered as she tried to remember the event that had put her here in this hospital bed. She started shaking uncontrollably as the memory of that horrible night returned to her. She looked around for her mother, but the chair on the opposite side of the room was empty. She tried to turn to reach for the call button, but fell back onto her pillow as the searing pain slice through her left side. She gasped as beads of sweat mixed with tears of pain poured down her face. She must have let out a cry as a nurse came rushing into her room and asked her if she was all right and if she wanted something for pain. Lively managed to croak, "Where's my mother?" It was a rasping whisper, but the nurse understood. She said, "Your mother and father are down in the cafeteria."

Lively looked at nurse as if she had taken leave of her senses. What did she mean, her mother and father? She must have mixed her up with some other patient on this wing. Then the nurse continued. "I'll call down to the cafeteria and have them paged to let them know that you are awake. In the meantime the doctor has prescribed some pain medication for you and I will bring it to you in a few minutes." She turned and hurried from the room. Lively watched her go, then turned back to the window. What had that nurse meant when she said her mother and father? Then Lively began to wonder again about the stranger who had been in her room with her mother. The handsome stranger with the crystal eyes? It seemed that he and her mother were very well acquainted. She hadn't missed the tender, concerned looks that had passed between them. Was this someone from her job? Maybe he was a detective or policeman. That was it. He was waiting to question her when she awakened and was coherent enough to answer his questions.

While she was pondering all of this, she heard someone enter the room. She turned her head and saw Randy standing at the side of her bed. He had a big basket of fruit with a balloon tied to it that said "Get Well Soon." He also had a crystal vase with a single red rose in it. She knew that this was the rose he had given to her on her birthday.

He smiled at her, but she did not miss the pain and worry in his eyes. He leaned over and kissed her on her forehead and set the basket and vase on her bedside stand. She looked into his eyes as she tried to smile, but winced at the pain in her face. He sat sown on the edge of her bed and said quickly, "Don't try to talk. I know that you probably have a lot of questions and I will try to answer them as gently as I can, okay?" She gave him what she hoped was a nod and waited for him to begin.

He lifted her hand to kiss it as he began. "When I left you at your house the other night, I just felt like something wasn't quite right. I couldn't put my finger on it. I wanted to turn and come back, but I needed an excuse to knock on your door at that time of night. I didn't want to frighten you or your mother and grandmother unnecessarily. Then I remembered that you didn't have your flower vase that I had given to you for your birthday, so I hurried back to Hoppy's to get it. I was just turning onto your street when I saw some strange movements down by your house. I was too far away to see exactly what was happening, so I just kept walking at a normal pace. When I got to your house, though, I kept hearing sounds coming from that tall grassy field next to your house. It sounded like constant thudding and groaning. I put the vase down on the steps and slowly and quietly made my way toward the sound. When I reached the clearing, it took a few moments for my eyes to adjust to the scene in front of me because the moon had gone behind a cloud. When the cloud cover had passed and I could see again, I almost died. I saw you lying on the ground and Curtis Sampson...."

His voice broke as he thought about what he had seen that night. He took a deep breath and continued. "When I saw what he was doing to you and then I saw his hand come down toward you with a knife, I lost all control. I grabbed him and I saw red as I pounded him over and over again. Your mother must have heard the commotion as she walked home, because she and some white gentleman came bursting into the field and the man grabbed me to stop me from killing Curtis. Curtis was on the ground writhing and cowering and babbling incoherently, but we could make out some of his words. He was begging his father to stop beating him, that he didn't mean to be bad and he would go to the cellar. We didn't have time to worry about him. Your mother was screaming and the gentleman with her was yelling for me to call and ambulance and the police and when they arrived, they hauled Curtis away, still babbling about how he had loved you since kindergarten. You were rushed by ambulance to the hospital and sent straight to surgery. You had severe internal bleeding going on and they needed to stop that right away. You are a very lucky lady. I'm so glad that I followed my feelings and came back. If I hadn't...."

He couldn't finish the sentence. He broke down sobbing. At that moment, her mother and the man came into her room. They saw Randy standing by her bed crying and the tears rolling down her cheeks and realized that she knew the reason for her being in the hospital. Her mother gently lifted her and cradled her in her arms as she had done when Lively was a little girl. She began crooning to her that she would be all right, that Mama was here and nothing would hurt her again. The tall man and Randy looked on silently.

After Lively had stopped sobbing and her trembling had subsided, Mama gave Randy a knowing look. He politely excused himself and left the room. Mama gestured to the man to come stand beside her. She looked lovingly at him and then turned back to Lively.

She took a quivering breath, and said, "Lively, honey, I'd like for you to meet someone that I've known for many years. His name is Greg Franklin, Jr.." The man and Mama looked deeply into each other's eyes and Lively saw the burning love that radiated between them. She knew even before Mama said the next words. "Greg Franklin is your father."

CHAPTER THIRTEEN

Lively was sitting up in bed staring out of the window. She didn't see the green leaves on the tree outside of her window, or the pair of birds building a nest in one of the branches. Her mind was still whirling with the news her mother had shared with her earlier. She didn't know what to feel and right now all that she felt was numbness. She had met her father. All of these years she had wondered about him. She had thought that he might be dead and it was too painful for her mother to talk about it to her and that is why they always told her that they would tell her about him when she was "old enough". She had pictured a handsome man with a light caramel complexion, which would explain the lightness of her skin. She knew he would be tall and large-framed, because she was a large-boned girl and Mama and Grandma were more on the petite side. She didn't know what to feel about this white man who was her father. He seemed pleasant enough and he certainly was successful. Mama had told her that he was a lawyer and was here to take over his father's practice because the elder Greg Franklin was retiring. But, there were a thousand unanswered questions running through her mind causing her head to ache. Just as she was about to ring for the nurse, Greg Franklin walked in. He was alone. She wondered where Mama was, but before she could ask, he answered her question.

"I asked your mother to go home and get some rest. She has been here around the clock for three days and she is just about worn to a frazzle. Besides, I wanted a chance to talk to you because I know you are confused and shocked to learn that I'm your father."

Lively stared at the stranger. He certainly was a handsome man. She could understand how Mama had fallen for him. She was just confused as to his feelings about her mother and her. How did they meet and fall in love? How come they didn't marry? Why was Mama left alone to raise her while he went on with his life that had obviously been one with more comfort and luxuries than she'd had? She found herself feeling some slight resentment toward him. Her feelings must have shown on her face, because Greg Franklin quickly said, "Before you condemn me for all the years that I was not around, I need to tell you why I wasn't there." He spoke softly but not apologetically. He did not act ashamed or intimidated. He looked straight at her. Lively recognized a determined set to his jaw and was shocked when she saw some of her own features reflected in his face. This was her father!

"I met your mother when she came to work for my parents," he began. "I remember the day so well. I opened the door in answer to her knock and there she stood. She was so beautiful, but she looked like a scared rabbit. I think that I actually lost my heart to her at that moment. She looked up at me with those beautiful frightened eyes and I don't know, something happened to my heart. I took her in to meet Mother for her interview and stayed in the room to hopefully give her some measure of comfort. After Mother hired her and she started working for us, I would see her scurrying about the house like a frightened mouse. I don't think she ever got over her fear of Mother and she generally stayed out of our way. I wasn't home most days because I was attending the junior college here in town. When

I was at home, we began talking and sharing thoughts and I really enjoyed those times with her. I found her to be very smart and interesting to talk to. She had a wonderful sense of humor, and she was a great listener. The day that I knew that I was in love with her was an evening that I was driving out to the college to pick up some schoolwork and I saw her walking home. The sun was just setting and a light breeze was blowing her soft hair around her face. I pulled up beside her and when she saw me, I saw her eyes light up and color creep into her cheeks. She looked so young and vulnerable that I wanted to hold her in my arms and keep her safe." He paused as his mind raced back to that time. He had a sad smile on his face as he continued. "We started seeing each other whenever we could, but didn't let anyone know about our relationship. My parents would have objected and I didn't want to subject your mother to any recriminations from my mother. When we learned that your mother was pregnant with you, we knew that we had to tell our parents. I wanted to marry your mother and take her away from here so that we wouldn't cause any problems for my father who was very involved in politics at the time. So, each of us decided to tell our parents and that's what we did. Your grandfather on your mother's side and my father came up with an agreement that your mother would continue working for them and my parents would pay for all of the things that you would need while I was in school. Then after graduation, I would marry your mother and we would raise you together." He sighed and looked at her. She was waiting to hear what had happened to cause him and Mama not to marry.

She didn't have to wait long. When he spoke again, his voice had lost its softness and had a hard edge to it. "After about a year in school, your mother's letters stopped coming. I kept writing to her, but never got any answers. Finally, I called my mother to ask what was going on. She told me that your mother was engaged to a man who lived in town and they seemed very happy together. I was broken-hearted. I buried myself in my books and studied very hard. I graduated ahead of my class with top honors. I never came back home to visit and eventually met someone and we were married. We had two children, together, but the marriage was doomed from the start and we were divorced a couple of years ago.

Lively's brows were drawn together as she pondered her next question. "Why didn't Mama try to contact you after you had stopped writing? Didn't she want you to know about me, when I was born and how I was doing all these years?" she asked, the hurt making her voice sound like a little girl.

Greg saw that she was hurt, so he hastily explained. "Of course she did, but my mother had done a good job of convincing her that I had fallen in love with someone else and began intercepting our letters to each other, so your mother assumed that it was over between us and never tried to contact me again. Then a few months ago, your grandfather, my father, contacted me to tell me that he was retiring and wanted me to take over his law office. I thought about it for a while, and decided to take a trip here to decide if I would like to take over the practice. On my first day home I saw your mother walking toward the house. I hadn't seen or heard from her in over sixteen years. When we looked into each other's eyes, we knew that we had never stopped loving each other. We talked and that's when we discovered my mother's treachery. After your mother left work for the day, I confronted my mother about her deceit and she admitted everything. I left her house and am staying at the inn and have been seeing your mother again. We had decided to wait until your birthday to tell you about me. That is the reason I was with your mother the night we found you and you ended up here. I was coming home with her to explain all of this to you. I wanted you to know that I never left you or your mother intentionally. I loved you both from the start. Over the years I would ask my mother about you and she would tell me that you were happy with your new father, so I always felt it best not to interfere with your happiness. I'm so sorry that you had to suffer from my mother's deception." He stood up and leaned over the bed as if he wanted to take her into his arms, but decided against it. He felt it was best to let this entire story sink in and hoped that in time she would forgive him. She saw tears glistening in his eyes and she began to cry softly. Even though her father was a stranger to her, she still felt a tug at her heartstrings for this kind and gentle man and for her mother who had been denied the pleasure and freedom to love one another. She thought about Randy and herself. How it had almost been unbearable waiting just two months until she turned sixteen. How lonely Mama must have been all those years. She remembered all of the times she had seen her mother with a faraway sad look in her eyes. Was it because she had been mourning for her first and only love? Now she knew why Mama always told her that she was a gift of love.

And what about Grandma? Had she known about her father all along? Was this the reason for the polite silence that was always between Mama and Grandma? Lively had so many questions. She looked at her father. He was looking at her speculatively as if he wanted to say more. He realized that she had a lot of information to digest and needed time to be alone so he stood and with the promise of seeing her again the next day, he left the room.

She turned over and lay looking out of the window. She didn't know what to think. She finally had a father like her friend Janelle and like Randy. He was well-to-do like their fathers, too. Finally the mystery was solved. She began to understand now why Mama and Grandma never told her about her father. They had been sworn to secrecy by her two grandfathers. Lively wished her grandpa had not died when she was a little girl so she could ask him how he could have just given in to Mr. Franklin's proposal without thinking about how Mama felt. She could never tell him about the loneliness and shame she had felt all of her life not knowing who or where her father was. And what about her paternal grandparents? She had been to the huge house several times with Mama when she was small. She had seen the stern-looking white haired lady and the tall man when she was there. They had been kind to her, but never acknowledged by their actions that she was their grandchild. And what about Randy? Did he know? Was that the reason for his sudden departure from her room when he and Mama had nodded to each other? She had so much to try to understand. Exhausted from all of these uncertainties, she fell into a fitful sleep.

CHAPTER FOURTEEN

Lively Jones Franklin Simmons sat on the steps of her childhood home enjoying the midsummer evening breeze. She watched the two children tossing the green ball back and forth and hearing the childish giggles as they tried to toss the ball high into the air and catch it in their small hands. She looked over at her husband, Randy as he stood beside a shiny new Mustang convertible that belonged to her mother. Her father was standing next to him and they were deeply engrossed in conversation about a well-known court trial that was taking place in New York City. It was a class action suit brought against a company that kept refusing to promote African-Americans to supervisory positions. She heard the front door open and close and turned to see her mother carrying a tray with a pitcher of lemonade and crystal glasses on it. She looked at Lively and smiled. Mama looked even more beautiful than she had five years ago when she and Greg had come to visit them in New York when Lively was expecting her second child. Lively had taken a few years off from her career as a buyer for a large department store in New York to be a full-time mom so she spent the time with Mama and getting to know her father. He had been so kind and gentle that she did not find it hard to accept him into her life. It was a strange situation, at first. People would stare at them and some were downright rude in their comments but her father had a way with words and such an engaging smile and personality that he soon had won the whole neighborhood over. All she heard now were words of praise and respect for "Mr. Greg" as he was called. And despite his gentle manner, you would never know that he was the same aggressive attorney who fought doggedly for his clients in the courtroom. He had represented her when Curtis Sampson went to trial for the assault on her. In the end, Curtis was declared criminally insane and sent away to a state across the country to a mental institution, and he was still there to this day.

Lively looked at Grandma dozing in the old rocker in the corner of the porch. Grandma slept a lot these days. Her white hair was pulled into a bun at the nape of her neck and her face was an array of lines, but you could see the beauty that had once been there. She still had a mischievous sparkle in her eyes when she talked to you. Lately, she had begun to tire very easily and because she had suffered a stroke, she had to use a cane to get around. Most of the time she was content just to sit in her rocker and sleep. It was hard to believe that this wizened lady had been embroiled in an affair with a powerful political figure that nearly cost him his career and his family. Lively had learned about all of this a few years ago after Mama and her father had married. She finally had to courage to approach Grandma on the subject of why she never told her about her father and why she had not stood up for them against Mr. And Mrs. Franklin when they had wanted to marry. Grandma was hesitant at first, but then as if a dam burst open, she poured out the story of her love and affair with Greg Franklin, Sr.. They had been deeply in love. The affair went on secretly for about four years. A child was conceived from that relationship, then Mrs. Franklin found out about the affair and demanded that he end the affair immediately or she would expose him and ruin his career. He did as she demanded. Myrtle was fired and forced to have an abortion and although he loved her, Mr. Franklin loved being a politician more. She had tried to keep the Franklins at a distance, so that the story of her affair would not leak out again after all of these years. But, then history had repeated itself when her daughter had started seeing Greg Jr. Then, when Ella had gotten pregnant and her grandpa Jones found out, he was livid. He said he thought he was through with the Franklins and their involvement in their personal lives.

"So, once again, we were sworn to secrecy and thought it better to not let anyone know that you were the grandchild of Senator Franklin. We did it to keep you from the scrutiny of this small town," she explained.

Lively had a chance to meet her paternal grandparents a few years ago. They had come to New York on business after the birth of her daughter. They had called her to see if it was okay to stop by to see the baby. Lively refused, but later Randy, in his gentle patient way convinced her to let them come over. Lively felt very nervous as she waited for them to arrive. She was also afraid, angry and hurt. She was still bitter with them for never having acknowledged her when she was growing up almost in their own backyard.

When the doorbell rang and Randy escorted the old couple into the den, all of her bitterness faded as she looked at the withered lady and stooped man twirling his hat nervously in his hands. She smiled graciously at them and sent Randy to the kitchen to make them some tea. She got up and went to the nursery to get the baby. The old lady reached for the baby with shaking hands and Lively gently placed the child in her arms. She told them that her name was Lauren Elizabeth after Randy's mother and grandmother. They stayed for an hour and when they left, they hugged Lively and through the tears in their eyes, she knew they wanted her forgiveness. She looked at them and said, "Thank you for stopping by, Grandma and Grandpa." She saw their eyes light up and knew that everything would be fine.

The old homestead had changed over the years since Mama and Greg had gotten married. It had been totally rebuilt and repainted. The tiny rooms had been enlarged and extra rooms added on. There was now a den and a study for Greg with all of his law books in a bookcase that covered one entire wall. The desk in the center was massive and made of rich, dark oak. There were two large brown overstuffed leather chairs in the room and expensive oil paintings garnished the walls. The living room had been expanded and completely refurbished. The walls had expensive beige and white striped wallpaper covering them. There were two large leather white sofas facing each other in the room. A beautiful glass cocktail table sat between the two sofas. White and cream oil paintings hung on the walls giving the room a regal look. A white baby grand piano with a large ivory bust on it sat in one corner of the room. The floors of the house were covered in plush white carpeting. The kitchen was now a large airy room with stainless steel appliances and white Spanish tile on the floor. There was a circular bar-style breakfast nook in the corner of the room. A patio had been added at the back of the house leading from the kitchen. There was a little stone footpath leading from the patio to a gazebo by a cement waterfall. All along the footpath were wildflowers in so many colors that it was hard to distinguish what varieties they were. The front and back yard had grass so thick and green that it looked almost surreal. Mama had told her that it was designed to resemble the place where she and Greg Jr. had fallen in love. Lively knew from the way she said "love" that this is where they had made love to one another. But, she didn't want to embarrass Mama, so she never mentioned it.

Lively looked at the two children playing in the yard. The boy who was four was tall and sturdy like Randy. He was so like his father in other ways, too. He was such a kind and loving child, soft-spoken and intelligent. The little girl was six. She had her mother's caramel complexion, long curling ringlets that softly encircled her heart-shaped face. When she smiled, two deep dimples appeared in her cheeks. She had a lively spirit that kept everyone laughing at her antics. She was the apple of her grandpa Greg's eye. He affectionately called her "little Hunny."

Lively saw Randy turn toward her and smile, then head off to play with the children. He was such a good father. Greg climbed the steps and as he passed, laid his hand on her shoulder, and then continued up the steps to stand by her mother, who was watching the children play. He put his arm around her waist and smiled a smile of happiness and contentment. Mama looked up at her husband with all of her love for him shining in her eyes. Circumstance had kept them apart, but fate and an undying love had brought them full circle back to each other.

Lively felt her heart bursting with happiness and as her eyes began to well with tears, she stood up and walked down the steps toward the street. She saw a piece of paper spinning and tossing by as it was whipped up by a whirlwind. She smiled to herself as she watched it whirl out of sight. She turned and hurried back to her family.

ABOUT THE AUTHOR

La Juanda Huff Bishop was born in Commerce, Texas a small town east of Dallas. When she was two years old, her father who was in the Army was transferred to a military camp in California. From that point on, the family would spend the next fourteen years living in different states and countries such as Alaska, Maryland, New Jersey, Georgia, Germany, Washington, Louisiana and Arizona where La Juanda presently lives with her husband, Theodore.

She has always been an avid reader and at the age of thirteen started writing short romance stories to share with friends and classmates. But, it was not until the tragic loss of her oldest daughter, Anita, that La Juanda began to take her writing seriously. She says that this was a gift given to her from God in exchange for her daughter.

La Juanda is fluent in German and she says she can dabble in Spanish if necessary. She has written a collection of poems entitled *God, Birds, Bees, People and Trees*, a novel, *Lively* and is currently working on a new novel.

In addition to writing, she enjoys reading, camping, fishing, gardening and making crafts. Above all, she says that she enjoys life.

Printed in the United States
17133LVS00006B/4-54

9 781413 714753